GW01458522

Please return this book on or before the date shown above. To renew go to www.essex.gov.uk/libraries, ring 0345 603 7628 or go to any Essex library.

Essex County Council

Dedication

To Victor Stuart, a real life character and inspiration for this adventure

G N STUART

SPOILS OF WAR

AUSTIN MACAULEY PUBLISHERS™

LONDON · CAMBRIDGE · NEW YORK · SHARJAH

A CIP catalogue record for this title is available from the British Library.

ISBN 9781398408999 (Paperback)
ISBN 9781398409002 (ePub e-Book)

www.austinmacauley.com

First Published (2021)
Austin Macauley Publishers Ltd
25 Canada Square
Canary Wharf
London
E14 5LQ

Part 1
September 1991 Manchester

Chapter 1

Before he even opened his eyes, his head was throbbing. It was supposed to be a quiet night out – just as a warmup for his 21st birthday party that evening. But of course, like most of their family celebrations, it didn't stay quiet. Everyone went too far, resulting in a rough start to a day that would go on long into the night with celebrations.

It was Uncle Charlie as usual, always the one to get the party started. As they walked into the first pub from the back of the line, they heard, "Eleven pints of lager and eleven cigars please landlord!" And that was it. Everyone was obliged to shout their corner so at least eleven pints had been drunk, and he remembered a few spirits as well. Also, the cigars came back to recollection due to the rank state his mouth felt in. God knows what he would sound like today. A cigar was always something that seemed a good idea at the time, but he regretted it the next day.

He looked at his watch. Nine minutes past one in the afternoon. Didn't see much of the morning then! But that was the beauty of having his own place and living on his own by his own rules. No one really to please and if he wanted to sleep in all day at the weekends, who cared, certainly not Glenn, to be honest who would even know. Glenn Mulligan had been living on his own for about six months now after plans to move in with his girlfriend of three years went pear shaped. He never could work out why or whose fault it was; talking to friends and people at work that seemed to be the norm. Blokes just didn't get the subtleties of relationships and, therefore, couldn't see when they were going wrong and generally always acted too late to do anything about it. Well, that was his experience anyway.

After buying a place together and spending time, effort and money he didn't have, trying to create the love nest they had talked about, he got the 'Dear John' phone call. The call that said, "I think I have made a mistake, I don't want to settle down; well, not with you anyway!" And that was it, nothing he could do about it no matter how he tried. It was a rocky few months, but he pulled himself together and got through it.

So, time to move on. He bought her out, took on the full mortgage on his own, and against most family advice, moved out of the family home and set up in his own place. He wasn't well off but had enough money to cover the bills: about £15 a week for food – not bad for a single guy, especially if you threw in a few family scrounged weekly meals and he had come to get the shopping down to a fine art. Single man-sized tins of beans all the way! The rest went on various nights out. In fact, he was always out and only stayed in one night a week, which made for a really hectic lifestyle. Just the way he liked it. No time to sit around feeling sorry for yourself.

Work wasn't too stretching. He worked in a personnel department for a large FTSE100 company, mainly staffed with women, which wasn't the worst office to work in! He wasn't too ambitious and, therefore, life was pretty good. No women in his life but everything else was turning out OK.

He pulled on jeans and a jumper and stumbled his way downstairs and into the kitchen to switch on the kettle. He desperately needed a brew. Looking in the fridge, he had a couple of slices of bacon and some bread. That would do nicely; smothered in brown source would either make or break him. It always had to be brown, he could never understand people who ruined a bacon butty with red sauce. His younger brother, Brian, was one. He knew he wouldn't have any paracetamol in the house so would have to grab them from Mum and Dad's later.

He flicked on 'Grandstand' while he ate although it never seemed the same since they replaced Des Lynam with Steve Rider. As far as he could remember, if he wasn't going to the football himself, Saturday afternoons were usually watching sport on Grandstand before final score came on. Fond family memories those Saturday evenings. Now of course final score was just the lead up to getting ready and going out on the town.

But not tonight. Tonight was his 21st birthday party. Was he looking forward to it? He never really liked to be the centre of attention when it was about himself. At one of these team building things they do at work, someone described him as an introverted extravert. Happy to be the life and soul of the party if the focal point wasn't about him. He liked that; it fitted his personality. But tonight, it was all about him. His game plan was to just play it cool, not get too drunk too early and leave the heavy drinking for the after party back at Dad's. They had hired a DJ called Crazy Colin, who said he would do a bit of an act on stage and Glenn was happy to get involved for a bit of a laugh.

Chapter 2

The local conservative club was not the most glamorous of locations, but it held about a hundred and twenty people and was, therefore, perfect for the occasion. It also served the best pint in town, Boddingtons! Glenn's evolution from drinking underage pints of lager to what he now considered grown up drinking, Boddingtons Bitter was just the job.

The place was filling up quite nicely. There was the corner with the wider family, aunts and uncles you only saw for weddings, funerals and that sort of thing. Glenn was lucky his wider family was brilliant and always brought a raucous sense of fun to any gathering. Next to them were his work colleagues. He was chuffed as over 20 of them had made the effort. The rest of the room was filled with friends, neighbours and more family. He had three pints already lined up but remembering the game plan was taking it relatively steady.

He noticed his Granddad Victor, making his way across. What a character this guy was. Loved by all the guys in the family but hated by the women who just saw him as the family drunk. Glenn loved that though as he just didn't give a damn. From what he knew, every job was just a way of making money, to get out to the pub and get plastered. He smiled as he remembered his dad telling him a story of an occasion he came home drunk, which he usually did, and fell asleep on the toilet with a cigarette dangling out of his mouth. His long-suffering wife opened the door shouting, "Jesus, Victor, you're on fire!" in her thick Dublin accent before throwing a cold bucket of water over him.

Glenn felt it was easy for people to judge people like Victor, but he admired the life that generation had led. Victor Mulligan grew up in relative poverty in Dublin, before joining up and going through the war and then trying to bring up a young family through the harsh realities of North Manchester in the 50s and 60s. Good on him. Having said that, he was a great guy to have a drink with until he got to four or five pints and he then became a bit of a pain in the arse. For that reason, Glenn liked to get a beer in with him early doors and really enjoy his company.

"Hiya, Granddad how are you doing," he said.

"Hi there, Glenn, how are you?" replied Victor in his familiar Dublin accent. "Let's get a couple of pints; now you are a real man. In fact, let's get a little Bells Whiskey chaser with those. Here's a tenner get them in, Glenn, and I will grab us a table."

Glenn hated whiskey but Victor always insisted. He did the same thing every time, drank about half the pint and then poured the whiskey in. Glenn had never seen anyone else do that and wondered where that habit had developed.

"Ahh sit down, Son, I want to talk to you," said Victor.

"Oh yeah, Granddad what about?"

"I have been waiting for this day for a while to speak to you about something from the past. My past. Pass those drinks over."

They sat down towards the back of the room near the bar.

"Now listen. I want to tell you a story. Can't really do it here as it's quite a long story relating back to the war and an adventure we got ourselves into in the desert. So, let's talk again tomorrow. Do you promise me, Son, you will come around tomorrow? Now it's very important."

"Sure, Granddad although I might be a little rough though judging by how tonight's going."

"Ah, you bloody kids you have no stamina, wet the lot of you, Jesus! So, I wanted to tell you a story about bout how me and a couple of me mates buried some treasure. It's still there as far as I know, and I want you to go and get it. Are you listening to me, Son?"

"Treasure, Granddad are you winding me up?"

"No, your cheeky little bastard. Come around tomorrow and I will tell you all about it."

"All right," said Glenn. "I will be round in the afternoon."

Just then Crazy Colin, the very strange DJ, announced the show was going to start. Glenn knew this was his cue to finish his pint with Victor and go up on stage.

"OK, Granddad I need to go up now but will catch you tomorrow," said Glenn.

"Ahh, Son, you will," said Victor on his way back to the bar.

Glenn shook his head and wandered over to where his brother stood just next to the little stage. All the young kids had gathered around the stage and were sat on the floor waiting to be entertained.

"All right kid," said Brian. "What did Granddad want then?"

"Even for Victor Brian, this was a strange one. He said he buried some treasure in the war and now that I am a man, he wants me to go and get it. Can you believe that?"

"That's a classic one, mate, he must have shot the whiskey early tonight," said Brian, chuckling.

Just then, the curtains opened and there stood Crazy Colin on a chair stark bollock naked!!! Well, he would have been but for the rubber chicken on his genitals before he started singing to the music, "'Has anyone seen my cock?'"

"Oh shit," said Glenn.

The place erupted with parents diving to the stage to pull their children away!

Chapter 3

For the second day running, Glenn's hangover was head splitting! But what a night. God knows what time he got to bed but it must have been a late one. His head was absolutely ringing until he realised it was the phone. He picked it up.

"Glenn, is that you, your lazy bugger?" came an Irish accent.

"Yeah, Granddad you woke me up. Got a cracking hangover from last night mate."

"It's nearly 3 in the afternoon and I have been waiting for you to come around. Get your arse round here, I want to talk to you," said Victor.

"OK, Granddad give me half an hour. Brian's coming as well so will pick him up on the way. See you in a bit."

"Ah, OK Son, I will put the kettle on," Victor said as he replaced the receiver.

Glenn dragged his backside out of bed and got dressed after a quick wash that hardly made him feel human again.

Bloody Victor he thought, *what the heck is he banging on about now and why it couldn't wait at least until he had a clear head?* He would go around there, talk to him and be back in bed in an hour. He drove the five minutes or so around to his family home and let himself in the back door.

"Hello only me," he said as an announcement of his presence. The place looked like a bomb had gone off. Cans and bottles all over the place with plates of food and leftover pizza here and there. Nothing he didn't expect. The family parties had become legendary affairs and when last orders rang at the venue, it was all catered for back at the house. To be honest, the after-parties were always better and deep down, he knew it would continue later today although his body was telling him something else! Good job he booked the day off work on the Monday.

He made his way into the front room through the kitchen. There was the familiar site of his dad, in his chair reading the morning paper. His dad was a man of ritual and every morning he wasn't working, he would be sat reading the papers. Having said that, it was late afternoon so the old man must be suffering a bit as well from last night.

"Hi Dad," he said.

"Hi Glenn, surprised to see you up so early! What a cracking night that was. Where did you get that DJ from? Bloody hell he was something else, wasn't he? Your mum's none too chuffed he was a bit rough and ready for some of the family, but I thought he was bloody brilliant!"

"Yeah never seen anything like that before, Dad. It was certainly memorable. I said to him before the night I would get up and have a bit of a laugh with him in his show. Have to say I shit myself when he came on stage. Luckily though, I think I got off lightly."

"Reckon you did, mate. Good night though. Anyhow, Charlie and Lisa are coming down about five o'clock, I have invited a few friends round to help sup up the rest of the beer that's left over, so good job you came around to help us clean-up."

"Oh no, somehow I knew you would say that! I will be here but just picking Brian up as Granddad wants to have a quick word with us this afternoon. So, will be back in half an hour," Glenn said as he made his way back to the kitchen in search of paracetamols. A couple of tablets later, and a glass of water, he walked back into the living room shouting up the stairs to Brian to get a move on.

"What's your granddad want then?" said Dad. "He was reasonably well-behaved last night, left about midnight in a taxi, but he had definitely had enough to drink."

"Don't know, Dad, just think he wants a chat on our own. You know we don't go around enough, and I think the old guy just wants to make that point."

Just then Brian came down the stairs, looking even worse than Glenn felt. He grabbed his coat without saying anything and headed out the back door. Glenn followed him.

"See you in a bit, Dad," said Glenn.

They got in the car and headed off for Granddads.

"What about that frigging DJ last night?" said Brian. "Thought he was going to have your pants off, mate."

"So did I! Got away with that one I reckon in the end."

"Cracking night though. Definitely need a hair of the dog today. I'm feeling like crap. I can tell you and can do without a fantasy story from Victor, that's for sure. Let's go and see what the old bugger has to say. What was it buried treasure from the war?"

"Yeah, he has told us some cracking stories over the years, most of which I believe, but I think treasure is pushing it a bit. Dad's invited everyone round again for tea so you will get your chance of more beer tonight."

"Great," sighed Brian.

They arrived at Victor's and let themselves in. Three cups of coffee were steaming away on the kitchen table and a packet of chocolate digestives. Victor came out of the bedroom all dressed up looking smart and obviously on the way to the pub.

"Hello boys, how's the heads? It's about time you got here," said Victor.

"Not great, Granddad," said Brian as they sat down and cracked open the digestives. Just the job for a sore head.

"You both look rough as toast. I'm going down to the pub, do you want to come along. Looks like you two need a drink more than me."

"No thanks, Granddad, we got to get back to mum's as everyone is coming around to crack on with the party. I guess you're not bothering with that then," said Glenn.

"No chance, Son; can't be doing with family gatherings, there too many women there for my liking. Right now, while you are filling your faces, let me tell you what I want to say. I have been writing down a few stories from my war years, but this is one I particularly want you boys to hear," he said as he was waving around what looked like a hundred sheets or so of paper.

"Bloody hell, Granddad looks like War and Peace, mate, we haven't got all day," said Brian, laughing.

"It's not quite finished yet but I just wanted to run it by you. As I said to Glenn last night, during the war me and a couple of mates stumbled over a German patrol in the desert. To cut a very long story short, we did them and found they were carrying all sorts of things. They were up to no good but among their cargo was a box of gold coins. They looked bloody old and we figured must be worth a fortune. Must have been a couple of hundred of them in this old lead box. We couldn't take them back so buried them up in the mountains around a place called Himeimat. We got in a few scraps around there I can tell you. The plan was to go back for them after the war, but it was never the right time. As far as I know, they are still there and that's what you boys need to get your arses in gear and go and see if you can fetch them," said Victor.

Glenn and Brian looked at each other. "Gold coins in the desert; are you taking the piss, Granddad?" asked Glenn.

"Cheeky little bugger; no, it's straight up and genuine. When I have finished the full story and the details on where exactly I think they are, I will let you read it. It's no bullshit, boys, I promise you. Are you listening to me?"

"We are, Granddad, but you have to admit it sounds a bit fresh and where is this place anyway?" asked Glenn.

"North Africa, Egypt to be a bit more precise. We spent a few months out there in the battle of El Alamein. You must have heard about that."

"Africa," laughed Brian. "And how do you expect us to just trot off there and look for treasure – I bet we couldn't get the holidays and anyhow how much would something like that cost – I'm bloody skint at the moment."

"Boys, boys, it's a great adventure, and I can't bloody well go, can I? I have the money saved away so I will pay the expenses – I am not really interested in the money; it's just been bugging me all these years, is it still there? Can you imagine if it is? We will split any profits. What's there to lose?"

"Apart from our sanity you mean," said Glenn. "OK Granddad – let's have all the information and we can think it over – can't say any fairer than that now, can we!"

"All right, boys, that will do for me. Right, they will be wondering where I am down the George. I haven't been this late in there for years. Probably think the old bloke has finally croaked it."

"Yeah see you later, Granddad," said Brian as the door shut behind Victor as he moved remarkably quick on his feet. "Sounds like a load of old bollocks to me, Glenn, although wouldn't mind going to Africa, especially if Granddads paying."

"You have to have a load of injections you know," Glenn said laughing as he knew Brian hated needles.

"Bollocks to that then! OK, let's get back to Dad's; somehow we need to get the party started!"

Chapter 4

A couple of weeks had passed since Victor had shared his story with the boys. He wasn't so convinced they believed him, but he would try again now his story was complete. He had made an appointment at the solicitor's that morning. He had the idea for a fallback plan. If the boys didn't take it too seriously when he was alive, then he thought they would if they received the information from the grave! It was a bit morbid Victor knew that, but he couldn't help laughing to himself, wishing he was there when the solicitor gave the boys the story at the will reading.

He was sat in his chair by the patio door. Apart from in the George and Dragon pub, this was his favourite place to sit and contemplate life. He looked at the story he had been writing for the last couple of years. What a period of his life that had been. Taking him from Dublin to all sorts of places in the world. He remembered the tough life of Dublin and wondered if he had really made something of his life. He knew he hadn't, and he knew he had somehow wasted the chance he had been given by surviving the various scrapes he had gotten into in the war. He had lost a lot of good friends in those years.

Sure, he had managed to bring up two children and they had turned out as good as you could hope. Nice houses and nice families but if he was really honest, that was more down to their resilience and his wife's guidance rather than his role modelling skills. How had she put up with him all those years? She had died four years ago now and he missed her. It was no fun being on your own in the bungalow and that's why he took himself off to the pub. He liked talking to people. He had a big family around him, but they all had their busy lives, he understood that they meant well, but he was just down on their list of priorities.

He was proud of the work he had done writing his story. Probably the best thing he had ever done. Why didn't he start it years ago? Why didn't he find the time in the last half century to go back to that place in Egypt? Reading the story himself now, it didn't seem real it was so long ago. Great times with great blokes you could rely on. He hoped he had painted those characters in the way he thought of them. They deserved to be remembered as hero's as that's exactly what they were.

Heroes, he thought. He didn't feel much like a hero. *OK come on, you're a daft old sod,* he told himself, *no time to be miserable*. He sighed as he got up from his chair and made his way into the hallway.

A last look in the mirror, quick adjustment of his tie and he was ready to leave. He never left the house without looking top class smart even though around the house he looked like a bit of a tramp! The bus stop was literally twenty yards from the sheltered bungalows where he lived and, probably would die in. He was only seventy-two but the tough old life he had led had left him not in the greatest of shapes. His body was falling apart. He knew he could stop the fags and the booze but what was the point – might give him a couple more years of shuffling around in the bungalow.

The plan for the day was to ride the bus into town, do the solicitor's thing, he would then take in a couple of pints in the conservative club (he had never voted conservative in his life but the beer was the cheapest in town so Victor, in fact everyone, was willing to swallow their political allegiances for cheap good beer – at the last election, the conservatory candidate received 226 votes and there were over two thousand members of the Con Club!). He then planned to return home for a pork chop tea before going back out into the local pub.

The chop was sizzling away under the grill. Victor turned on the gas under the boiled potatoes and the cauliflower and thought about the day. Everything had gone to plan. The solicitor had made a couple of copies of his story. One that was in his bedside drawer and one the solicitor would present at a suitable time in the future unless the boys decided to act on it now of course, in which case he would tell the solicitor to bin the letter. In fact, he had given the solicitor a second letter with further instructions from the grave for that one!

There was a knock at the door.

Victor opened the door and it burst open; some kid had got him by the throat. He wasn't going to take that and punched the youth as hard as he could a couple of times and grabbed him round the head. He felt a big blow to his side as he realised there was a second youth! One, two, three, four blows and he had to let go of the first kid; he was now fighting for his life fifty years after he had done so many times in the war. Then he felt his shoulder go. His old wound from the war. His shoulder dislocated quite often, and it was a case of pushing it back in. A day or so's rest and it was always right as rain, so he had put up with the pain for years. As it went now, it took the strength from him.

"You bastards get out of my house," he screamed as another punch landed and knocked him over. He never felt pain like it – something had seriously gone wrong with his hip. He screamed again in pain. The kids ran into the front room, grabbed his wallet and turned and fled vaulting over Victor who lay in the hallway by the front door in agony. He saw them leave, clutching his wallet and actually smiled as he only had a tenner in it. *Hard luck, lads*, he thought, *you won't be getting very far on that.*

He then tried to move but his hip was screaming with pain and his shoulder was still out. He must have passed out and came too sometime later. It was a bit gloomier outside and the front door was still open letting in a chill on the autumn evening. No one must have heard the struggle but what must it have lasted 20 or 30 seconds and everyone in the bungalows were all deaf anyway! He couldn't stay here on the floor and tried to get up but there was no way. He must have broken his right hip and his right shoulder and arm lay limp. He was going to have to push that back in.

He wriggled around and got in a sitting position with his back to the wall. He brought his left-hand round and gripped his right arm, steadied himself and then pushed with all his weight, the familiar pain hit as the shoulder clicked back in place although it didn't seem as much as usual. He guessed that was because his hip was hurting too much to worry about his shoulder.

OK, what next? Raise the alarm. He could crawl out of the front door and try and attract someone's attention, but the bungalows were quite sheltered from the road and it could be a while before someone saw him on the floor. No, a better plan would be to crawl into the front room and reach the phone. He guessed it must have taken him about five minutes of movement and pain but sheer bloody will power got him there. He picked up the receiver and dialled 999, easiest and quickest number to dial.

"Emergency Services, which service do you require, fire police or ambulance?" he heard.

"Get me a bloody ambulance!"

Just then, the smoke alarm went off outside the kitchen. The chop was still under the grill and the bloody pans from tea were still on the cooker. "Better make that all three, love," he said through gritted teeth.

Chapter 5

Glenn was hard at work at his desk. The talk of Crazy Colin had died down in the office, but it still gave everyone a great laugh. He was writing up some minutes he had taken from the last meeting with the union. These meetings fascinated Glenn. It seemed to him, as a novice, that all the discussions that were held in the meeting had already been had before hand and that it all seemed very rehearsed even down to who asked what question and who responded. Well, above his head.

He loved the meetings though, the apparent 'them and us' mood when in fact they all really wanted the same thing. It did get him thinking that he reckoned his path lay down the management chain rather than the cause of the people. It seemed to make more sense to him. Setting the direction and putting forward the new ideas rather than simply responding to them and trying to get the best for their people from the idea's others had. Anyhow, it was just a feeling and got him thinking about where we might want the job to go. He might raise it at his next 121 meeting with his manager. As he was thinking that, the desk phone started to ring. Picking up and answered in his formal voice, "Glenn Mulligan speaking."

"Hi, Glenn, it's your dad. Bad news, mate. Someone tried to break into your Granddads flat, knocked him over and sounds like he has done his hip and shoulder again. I am on my way now but it's going to take me over an hour to get there, do you reckon you can knock off and get there quicker?"

"Jesus, Dad, I can't believe that. Yeah, I will get down there straight away, mate, and see what's going on." Even as he said this, he was saving his document and putting on his coat. "Where is he, do you know?"

"He's in infirmary in the A&E department."

"Right, I am on my way see you down there."

He was in the car in five minutes. If he was lucky and the lights were kind, he could be at the infirmary in 15 minutes, as he turned the first bend straight into the first set of red lights. He made it in just under 20 minutes and headed into the A&E department that even on a Tuesday afternoon seemed packed out. Having checked the board, it showed Victor in cubicle ten and he made his way in popping his head through the curtains.

"Granddad what the bloody hell has happened to you?" he said.

"Ah, Glenn, the bastards tried pushing in through the door. I put up a hell of a fight, but my shoulder gave way and the next thing I hit the floor. Think that scared them more than me as they did a runner."

"Jesus, are you all right?"

"Do I look bloody all right? I tell you twenty years ago, I have kicked their arses, biggest bloody mistake they would have made trying to force the way into my gaff. I tell you, Glenn, I would have given them the hiding of a lifetime and no more than they deserve."

"Who were they, any ideas?"

"Nah, just too bloody kids, didn't look that old. The police said they do that, prey on old people as they open the door. I should have had a chain on, but you don't think, do you on a Tuesday afternoon? Little bastards makes you blood boil."

"You are not wrong there for sure."

"Anyhow, they say I dislocated my shoulder again and may have broken my hip. I am dosed up more than those druggies you see hanging round the park. Shoulder goes all the time and it's just a case of pushing it back in, but my bloody hip is killing, Son, I can tell you."

"Are they taking you for an Xray and that then?"

"Yeah, at some point. Just waiting around at the moment for someone to take me down, but they are bloody busy today."

"Right. Dad rang me, he is on his way; should be here in 20 minutes or so. Think you gave him a bit of a fright, Granddad."

"He's not the only one. Tell you, Glenn, it's no fun getting old. I have always got into scraps and fights throughout my life, bloody hell fought the Germans in the war and they didn't get me, but that's the first time I felt hopeless. Do you know what I mean, Glenn?" Tears filled Victor's eyes. Glenn felt really sorry for him. Here was a proud old rogue who can't even open his own front door of an afternoon. Poor bugger.

"Well, let's hope they get the bastards and the get what they deserve."

"Police weren't too hopeful. They have taken fingerprints and all that, but no one saw anything, so they won't catch them," said Victor through gritted teeth as he tried to get comfortable in the bed.

A few hours later and they had settled Victor down in the ward. He had broken his hip so would need an operation and a long time to recover. He was going to have to get used to hospitals for a while. Everything that had to be said had been and it was one of those awkward periods by a hospital bed when everyone sat round not knowing what else to talk about while the poor guy who was ill just tried to get some sleep. Eventually, Glenn said his goodbyes and set off back home. He couldn't be bothered cooking now. *So I guess it would be another chicken satay from the Chinese on the corner.*

Chapter 6

Over the next month, there was the daily ritual of diverting his journey home after work to see Victor for half an hour before tea. He wasn't recovering well though and seemed to get more disillusioned as the days went by and suddenly developed pneumonia. You would think being in hospital was the best place when you are weak and recovering but Brian's theory was you are in with all the other patients who had god knows what and disease spreads around; certainly, it seemed like that for Victor anyway.

He called in on the Thursday night, but Victor didn't look too good. He had brought him a family-sized bar of chocolate but ended up eating much of it himself. Dad was already there, and he didn't look to good either.

"I am really worried about him, Glenn, he just looks so ill," said Dad.

"I know, Dad. Not a lot we can do. He is a tough old boot though if anyone can pull through, it will be Granddad," as he said that, Victor woke up.

"Hi boys can you get me a drink; I'm parched," said Victor.

"Sure, Granddad but its only water; they won't let you have any Bells in here," said Glenn, trying to lighten the mood.

Victor just shrugged as he took a sip of the water. He turned to Dad. "Son, am I going to die?" he said.

"I don't know, Dad, but you're very poorly," said Dad, taking hold of his hand. This little show of affection between the two of them really hit Glenn hard and he struggled to hold it together.

"Aye," said Victor and closed his eyes. He wouldn't open them again.

Glenn took the call at three thirty am and he knew what it was before he even answered it. Victor had passed, his Dad informed him. He sounded gutted.

"Sorry, Dad, this has all just been shit. I'm coming down."

When he got to Dad's, he was sitting up in his chair with a beer. That felt like the right thing to do. So Glenn grabbed a beer and joined him. Before long, most of the family were there, sharing stories of Victor and shedding a few tears as well. *All in all,* thought Glenn, *what a crap couple of weeks!*

The funeral all went off well as could be expected. There were a lot of long lost relatives from Dublin, so it was never going to be a quiet affair. It certainly was a celebration of his life and a chance for all the blokes to tell the stories of the bloke they knew as Vic and admired him for it. It was also a chance for a few of the wives to tell their stories with not such fond memories. But that was Vic! They all drank some Guinness, with a shot of Bells as a chaser pouring it into one glass when the pint was half full.

The surprise came a week or so later when the family went down to the solicitor's to hear the Will. No one expected much as he didn't have anything, so it caused a fuss when the solicitor said there is a very detailed letter there for Glenn and a sum of four thousand pounds to help Glenn carry out his wishes. *Four thousand pounds,* thought Glenn. *Where had he got that kind of money from*? For the last five years, his Granddad had been walking about in an old cardigan Glenn had given him. He must have been hoarding it rather than spending it. As he was thinking through this, he noticed everyone had turned to him and were looking for an explanation.

"This must be the story he told me about in the war and something he hid over in Africa. He asked me way back on my 21st to go out there and try and find it for him. I just thought it was one of Granddad's stories so never really took it too seriously. I suppose I had better read what he said and let you know what he wants me to do," said Glenn.

It took him a few days to read everything Victor had written down. It read more like an autobiography than a treasure map, but it was very intriguing. It was Saturday morning before Glenn had finished it. He needed to think it over and he did his best thinking while he was out running. He dug out his old trusty trainers and set off deep in thought. He was the only runner he knew, and friends used to say it must be boring just running for an hour not doing anything. But Glenn loved it – he could put the world to rights while pounding the streets.

The story sounded feasible to him. He couldn't do it on his own; Brian would have to be in on it. By the time he had done an hour and was approaching home, he had made his mind up. He would give the story to Brian to read. If he was up for it, then they would go for it. Bloody Africa, but what had they got to lose and even if they found nothing would have a great story to tell.

He dropped the paperwork off with Brian.

Brian settled down with a brew after tea and began to read Victor's story…

Part 2
May 1941 Dublin

Chapter 7

It was a late Friday afternoon, probably my favourite part of the week as work was drawing to a close. We would always meet the foremen in the 'The Five Lamps' pub to collect our weekly wages. It was always tough to stretch your money out through the week to the Friday. If it was a good week, you would get a Thursday night out; if not, that made Friday nights that much more enjoyable. I literally looked forward to Friday nights every hour I worked during the week.

I had a job as a labourer down at the docks. Not a very glamorous vocation but in these tough times, with the war in Europe raging all around us, you had to grab what you could. Labouring was very hit and miss. When the huge ships were in, there was plenty of work but there were weeks when ships were scarce. Fortunately for me, Uncle Jimmy was the 'Stevedore' for the company. These were the guys that had real power deciding who would get the work on any particular day. Not a job I could do, especially when he had to turn away blokes who literally had family at home going hungry. But someone had to do it; there wasn't enough work for all so these guys got to pick and choose. He always looked after me though and I pretty much had as much work as I could do.

I know he did it for me but also knowing that 20% of my wages went to my mother, the old girl being his sister. My mother's family never approved of Dad, married beneath her station and he would always be a hard worker but would never be anything more than a strong pair of hands. Jimmy loved him though and always went out of his way to look after our family as much as he could.

The docks were a tough old place to work, full of real hard blokes all working long hours for a living. I loved it and was probably fitter than any other point in my life. You didn't mess around and always pulled your weight as there was always a big bear of a hand waiting to give you a whack if you weren't doing your share.

I never shirked away from a scrap. I wouldn't say I was tough, more tenacious. I just never gave up and I guess the difference between fighters and non-fighters is that fighters don't mind getting punched in the face. My motto was always try and get more in than the other fella. But you didn't mess around down at the docks; there were some really hard bastards and they really could fight. We had a good crew though, always tried to work together in a gang and always looked out for each other. Some really great times with decent hard-working blokes.

This particular Friday was the last Friday of May and we were planning on making a night of it. Not like a Saturday night when I would put on my only suit. It was a light grey number and I thought that I looked like the bees knees. Ma said I looked like a 'Bloody American Gangster' that she had seen at the movies. That suited me, I quite liked that image. I just wished the girls did. It didn't really work with them if I was totally honest.

I got to the Five Lamps about five thirty, picked up my wages from the Super and got straight into the black stuff. I was meeting my mate down their Frank Gault, known to all of us as Franky Boy. He was a cracking lad and we had been best of mates for as long as I could remember. We literally did everything together. Matching suits the lot, although Franky had a real way with the ladies and always managed to have one or another on his arm. I always knew he had my back covered. It's rare and very valuable when you just know someone that well and it only comes from a relationship that had developed over years way back to school, short pants the lot.

Here he was late as usually with a big cheesy grin across his face. "Franky Boy, good to see you, mate," I said. "Are you getting them in?"

"Yeah, on my way, mate," he said. He ordered at the bar and then came over with two pints of Guinness and settled them down in front of me. He turned around and went back to the bar and returned with a couple of whiskeys!

"Good man," I said. "It's going to be one of those nights, is it?"

"Bloody long week, old pal, and I have a heck of a thirst. We have never been so busy. This war is cracking for business." I never really knew what he did. It was some kind of wholesale business selling stuff to the Brits and getting it transported across on ships. He seemed to be doing all right and like me always had some money in his pocket.

He took one huge swallow of Guinness, about half the pint, and then poured in the whiskey. I thought it is going to be one of those nights! And did the same. In fact, it became a bit of a ritual between the two of us after that whenever we had a chaser with a pint.

The night went off really well. The pub was full and had that Friday night feeling about it, with everyone in good spirits. It was drawing towards last orders, so we doubled up on our beer.

"I feel like a fraud, Franky Boy," I said. "The Brits are fighting for their lives over there against those Nazis and here's us carrying on as though nothing was happening. You're even making bloody money out of it."

"Hey steady on, old pal, I am just helping them with vital supplies they need. Supply and demand. They need it and I have it. You could say I was more than helping with the war effort."

"Yeah, well, I want some adventure. I want to pack all this in and get over there and fight some Nazis."

"You have been saying that for ages and never do it," said Franky. "You know me I am always up for an adventure. Reckon I would look pretty good in a uniform as well, be great with the ladies."

"Ha typical, Franky. Well, let's do it then. Get the next ship over there and join up. Two of my brothers are over there already as you know. Ma is not keen obviously, she goes mad when I mention it, but I can't sit on my hands any longer mate."

"Ah typical Vic always full of talk and bullshit," came a booming voice behind him. Big Micky was in his face a lot worse for wear. We never really got on and spent most of the time winding each other up whenever the chance presented itself.

"Shut the feck up, Micky, what's it got to do with you?" I said. "At least I have some scruples and want to help. You will keep your head down until the bloody Nazis march up the North Strand."

"Bollocks I will, but I don't see why we should throw our lot in with the Brits. They have never been nothing more than a pain in the arse for Ireland and always will be," said Micky.

"Micky, you are bloody clueless, mate. If those Nazis beat the Brits, we ain't got any hope. Do you think old Hitler's going to stop at the Irish sea? He's building an empire. Get a bloody grip, mate, and get you head out of your arse."

Big Micky was not called Big Micky in a comical way like some people call guys who are five foot tall. He was a bull of a man. Well over six feet tall and built like one of the tanker ships he serviced. So you didn't really want to mess with him but I had had a belly full of alcohol and was ready to take on the world. I didn't see his right fist; it came from nowhere and connected square on my chin. Next thing I knew, I was in the beer stains and fag ends on the floor around the bar. I looked up dazed and put my hand to a very aching chin. I saw Franky leap across the table and jumped on Micky's back. He was swishing him around like a rag doll. An area cleared around us and I was back on my feet, swinging with left and right arms and giving Mickey everything I had. It must have looked funny as hell with me and Micky trading punches while all the time he had Franky on his back grabbing at his face.

Suddenly, all three were on the floor and everyone was cheering and shouting and pissing us through with beer and anything else they could grab and throw on us. I felt a whack to the head from something very bloody hard and that brought me to a stop right away. It was the local bobbies. God knows how they got there so quick but there were four of them on us, giving us a good hiding with their truncheons. Jesus, they hurt but it brought the fight to a close to the disappointment of the crowd. They dragged us out into the street and carried on down to the station.

"A night in the cells will sober you lot of idiots up," said one of the coppers.

"Ah, come on, man, it was just a friendly end of week conversation; no need for that," I said but it had no effect and 10 minutes later, we had been booked in and thrown into a cell together! That always made me laugh. Maybe they expected us to beat the crap out of each other and save them a job. But by now, we had calmed down and sat about the cell feeling very sorry for ourselves.

"That's a hell of a right hook you have there, Micky," I said, rubbing my chin.

"Yeah, you didn't do too bad yourself there, Vic," he said, rubbing his eye. Franky just grunted, lay down and was asleep in seconds. It was going to be a long night.

Chapter 8

They let us out mid-morning and we made the walk of shame back through town in last night's clothes to explain to those at home where we had been. Ma was not going to be pleased as I hadn't been home to tip up my board. Dad would have kicked me up the backside had I not looked like I had already had a good beating at the hands of Big Micky and the police. They gave me a few harsh words but then it was over. They were good like that, didn't harbour grudges or let arguments drag on. They said what had to be said and then moved on. Ma knocked at the bedroom door towards teatime.

"Vic, are you going out tonight? Do you need me to press your suit?"

"Yeah, that would be great, Ma," I said with a very sheepish grin, "and I promise I will come home this time, unless I meet a nice girl down at the pub."

"There are no nice girls in the pubs you go into, my lad," she said as she picked up the suit and disappeared back through the door.

We were going out, Saturday nights as usual with the gangster suits on as Ma called them. Nothing special tonight, a trip round a few pubs and back to the Five Lamps for last orders. We always tried to end there as the landlord was relaxed and didn't worry too much about strict closing times, especially on a Saturday night – that's when he made most of his cash. Mind you, he might not be too happy about the previous evening, so I decided to go in there on my way to meet Franky and apologise for the night before. I figured that would go down well and ensure we didn't get barred later in the night.

It was a lively old night, had some really good laughs and our bruises from the night before were like medals of honour to the girls. We got back into the Five Lamps about 10:30 and loaded up on the beer to see us through a couple of hours. Luckily, the landlord was well up for a lock in, so we went on well into the early hours of the morning when there was the loudest bang I have ever heard, and we all hit the floor. Dust and debris everywhere. Before we could work out what was happening, there were more huge explosions hitting the town all around us. I scrambled to my feet and checked on Franky.

"You all right, mate," I shouted.

"Yeah, what the bloody hell is happening?" was his dazed response.

We gathered ourselves together and dashed outside as everyone else was picking themselves up. There were houses on fire all over the place, must have been hundreds of them. I could hear planes overhead and the realisation dawned on me we were being bombed. Had to be the bloody Germans but why had they bombed us in Dublin? We were keeping out of the war and trying to remain neutral. No time to worry about that now we had to help. We dashed down the road towards burning buildings and were met by Big Micky on the way.

"That's my bloody street on fire, boys, I need your help," he said.

We followed him around the corner and onto his street. I wasn't actually sure which one was his house, but he kept heading further down the street until he got to about three houses from the end. The house he approached and started to kick the door down on must have been his. It was a right mess. The roof had fallen in and it was ablaze. The heat kept pushing us back, but Micky braved it and went in. We looked around to see how we could help. People were running all over the place and a fire engine came screaming up the road. It stopped and hoses were unloaded and rolled out. We dashed over. "How can we help?" I said.

"We need water from the standpipes for the hoses but go to all the houses undamaged and get as many buckets as you can," said one of the firefighters.

"OK," I said, "but our mate has just gone into that house; he will need some help if you can get over there."

We legged it over to the houses on the opposite side of the street and tried a couple of doors before one opened. There was an old couple in there who looked frightened to death.

"We need buckets and water," I shouted, and they pointed me out to the yard. There were a couple of buckets full of coal which we emptied out onto the floor and filled them from the water butt. We went back inside the house and then dashed out through the front door back across the road to Micky's and went straight in through the door. I flung my water on the nearest flames I could see. Micky came out carrying what I presumed must have been his mother. Franky, who had come in behind me, saw them and threw his bucket right over them. We got them outside and took them across to the other house. Micky lay his mother down on the rug in the front parlour. She was coughing and spluttering which I took as a good sign, at least she was alive. We filled the buckets and made it back across the road as quick as we could. I just charged through the door and emptied my bucket on the flames. By this time, the fire brigade had a hose set up and were spraying through the upstairs window. As I came out again for another water run, Micky was heading back in.

A fireman grabbed his arm "Where are you going, you idiot, the place is about to fall down?" he said.

"My brother's in there, in the back room where the bomb hit. I have to get him out," said Micky, pushing him off and heading back inside. As he did, the back of the house collapsed and it was impossible to get in any further.

"We have to get the fire out, Micky, if we have any chance of getting your brother out," I said to him and dashed back to get more water. He joined in and we must have battled for about half an hour with the firemen before the house stopped burning. The collapse had actually helped douse some of the flames. The firefighters didn't hang around, they moved down the street tackling any fire they could see. Micky grabbed my arm. "You got to help me, Vic, my brother is in there."

"OK, lead the way, mate, but be careful, this lot could collapse at any time soon."

The three of us made our way into the house and started shifting the rubble. It took another hour of hard graft before we got to the back room and what looked like the bedroom which had collapsed through onto the ground floor. It was then we discovered the body of Micky's younger brother. It was a bloody awful scene and both me and Franky resorted to throwing up. Micky carried his brother out into the street and across the road. His mother had recovered now but started screaming and sobbing when she realised what had happened.

Micky just embraced her and sat down in the street with his brother and mother under each arm. It was a terrible scene.

Me and Franky were just exhausted and crumbled to the pavement next to them. We looked a right sight. The gangster suits were absolutely ruined, and I had burned some of my hair off. But it didn't seem to matter. We were alive and there must be plenty of people around that weren't. We sat there for what seemed like ages when Micky spoke.

"Vic, if you blokes are going to fight the fucking Nazis, then count me in, mate."

"Too bloody right I am; they ain't getting away with this. Franky, come on, mate, we need to help further down the street; we can sleep tomorrow," I said. "Micky, you all right here if we go?"

"Yeah, thanks fellas, I will never forget what you did for me tonight," he said, still clinging to what remained of his family.

With that, we got to our feet and trotted down the road with our buckets to where the firemen had just extinguished another fire.

Chapter 9

It had been a very long night. It had been the bastard Germans and that had turned the whole of Ireland against them. The latest news was that more than 300 homes had been damaged or destroyed including the Five Lamps; 28 people had needlessly lost their life and 90 people or so were injured and receiving medical treatment in hospital. It was incomprehensible. Why had they done it? We just couldn't get our heads round it. All those innocent people including Micky's brother. We were shattered by the whole experience. Life would never be the same again but one thing we had resolved to do was get across to Britain and join up as soon as we could and start fighting back. We had booked passage on a small boat heading to Poole in Dorset the day after Micky's brother's funeral.

There must have been a hundred people at the funeral. We had to get a bus out there to Ardmulchan Graveyard where Micky's family had some history. It was a very solemn occasion, a strange kind of summer day trip, a very weird experience in every sense. Anyhow, we gave him a deserved send off with the wake taking its toll on most of us, especially Micky, so it was a surprise to me when he came walking down the quay the following morning towards our boat and our ride to Britain and our entry into this war! I didn't know it then, but I was never to live in Dublin again after that departure.

The boat was carrying some unidentifiable cargo or another, so it wasn't exactly built for passengers, but we found ourselves some space and bedded down. This was my first taste of actually sailing on a ship having spent years offloading them, so I was feeling surprisingly excited about it. However, I naively thought it would be a couple of hours, we were on their nearly twenty hours and all three of us suffered with seasickness as soon as we got south of Ireland. God knows how those guys do it going back and forth across the Atlantic. Having took the mick out of them for years, I had to now admit what a hell of a job they do, but also made a pledge to myself that whatever lay ahead fighting the Nazis, it wouldn't be in the navy!

It was a beautiful summer's morning when the boat finally docked in Poole harbour and we were let off. It was a great relief to get back on dry land and our moods improved as we looked for somewhere to grab some breakfast before hunting down the recruitment office. We had no idea what we were doing but looking at the place, everyone looked like they had been in a war for a couple of years. Everything seemed geared to repelling the expected invasion from the enemy. It must have been like this for over a year since the famous withdrawal from Dunkirk. They looked like they could do with all the help they could get but yet they still seemed to have loads of spirit and fight left in them. You just had to admire the place and those first few minutes on the quay side really brought it home to me why we were here. We had to preserve our free way of life. This warm beautiful sunny morning in Dorset was almost perfect.

It wasn't the best breakfast I ever had but was appreciated all the same. It was good to fill my empty stomach after the crossing. We were pointed in the direction on the local army HQ which seemed to be some temporary kind of office set up in an old bakery. I supposed needs must in war, but I was expecting something a bit more impressive.

We met a Captain Smart and it appeared our luck was in as the Dorsetshire regiment or the 'Dorsets' as they all seemed to refer to themselves as, had been recruiting an 8th battalion to increase numbers and Captain Smart was forming some new platoons and we would fit the bill nicely. However, Captain Smart informed us that we were forming part of something called the 210th independent infantry brigade (home) with the emphasis on home. When we questioned this further, it was to be allocated to home defence, waiting to fight Hitler when he decided to invade.

Later, I asked the boys about it. "What do you think to this home defence malarkey then?"

"Doesn't sound to me like we will be doing much fighting, Vic, unless the Jerry's decide to invade. We could be sat around picking our arse for a while," said Franky.

"Yeah," said Micky, "and we don't really want those buggers trying it on over here. I thought after the battle of Britain stuff, they had fought that one off."

"I know," I said. "But they all seem to be still twitchy about it even though it was what over eight months ago before bloody Christmas."

"As I see it, it's a way into the army and getting our training under our belt. Who knows where it will take us, but we have to start somewhere. It's better than trapesing towards London, Vic, and looking for something else," said Franky.

"There's always the navy," said Micky with a rueful grin on his face.

"No bloody chance!" came a sharp chorus from me and Franky.

Basic training turned out to be a minimum of six weeks of drills, weapon training, route marches and what they called PT. Working down at the docks, we were all pretty fit so it didn't daunt us and didn't take us long to get fit as a fiddle. Our lodges weren't exactly plush as the three of us shared a tent, straw mattresses and a blanket. Some of the lucky blokes got sleeping bags but I never worked out how they swung that one. Food was pretty good though as I guessed they really did believe an army marched on its stomach. Not good as you kids would be used too but we got meat, or rather kind of meat cubes, loads of chocolate and spam!! We couldn't complain with this.

There were two particular bits of training we loved:

Weapons training – This was all new to us we had never even seen a gun before, let alone be allowed to fire them. Jesus, it was brilliant. We must have fired off thousands of rounds at targets and sometimes each other. They drilled into us to look after your weapon better than anything you have looked after in your whole life. If it worked, it could save your life, but you didn't get a second chance if the bloody thing failed. So we took that advice seriously enough!

The all in – This was a special favourite of all the lads as there didn't seem to be any rules. Sometimes at the end of a day of training, we used to do what the sergeant called an 'All in'. Basically, platoons used to face off against each other with the sole purpose of beating the shit out of each other. It was a great way to let off steam and really promoted the platoon spirit to get the upper hand. We loved it and there was no quarter given. It mirrored really the overall emphasis on hand-to-hand combat which during training we couldn't really fathom. If you had a machine gun, how would you end up getting close enough to grapple with the enemy? We later found out exactly why we needed the training and I reckon it saved my life on more than one occasion.

Once we finished our basic training, we formed back in our platoons and did platoon strategies and tactics for if, and when, we found ourselves in battle situations. So that was it, really 12 weeks or so of loads of lads having a great time training, eating, drinking and getting fit. We never even seen the enemy except for the bombers that occasionally flew over but the war and fighting all seemed as far away as it had been back in Dublin.

Chapter 10

Poole, Dorset June 1941

We were proud to be in the Dorset's and enjoyed settling into a routine of lounging around in the days and patrolling the coast at night. Although recently, we started approaching winter and the long dark cold nights and I have to say, you found it hard to find the fun in the patrols once the winter set in.

All three of us liked Captain Smart and to some extent, the sarge, but you would never admit that. Sargent Windle must have been in the army all his life. It seemed like the perfect job for him and he was definitely the bad cop in the partnership with the captain. To be honest, he probably ran things while the captain quite enjoyed the role of being the boss.

We weren't the most disciplined bunch so drove the captain mad at times, but we had a good deal of respect for each other and I think he particularly like us with our Dublin accents among all these Dorset tones. The problem was everyone was wound up and eager to see some action. We all watched the news reels of the war in the sky, the bombing of our cities and scuffles in various parts of the world but nothing seemed to be happening in England. Which on the one hand was good but if you asked anyone patrolling the coast, they were dying for Hitler to have a go, so we give him a bloody nose. We were convinced there was no way they could get past us.

One night, the three of us, who, by now, had been together day and night for over six months, were manning an observation post down by the beach. All routine nothing out of the ordinary.

"Jesus, it's cold," I said to no one specific. "I will get a brew on and try and warm us up a bit."

"Put some of this whiskey in it," Micky said handing me his flask. "I've also got some of those crappy biscuits left, might break your teeth off before you can eat 'em though."

"What teeth, you ain't got any left pretty boy?" I said playfully, slapping Micky around the jaw as we laughed and joked together.

Franky crawled over and whispered, "Hey, you two girls stop tickling each other up. I have just seen a bit of a light down there on the beach."

We started to take some interest and joined Franky with the binoculars looking across the bank onto the beach.

"I can't see anything, it's as dark as hell over there," I said.

"Shush and listen; I also heard something moving around," said Franky. You could detect the anxiety in his voice and Franky didn't spook easily so we were now on high alert.

We sat still as quiet as we could trying to piece the darkness with our eyes, but I just couldn't see anything. Just then, I heard a very quiet noise, but a definite noise made by someone moving, certainly not a natural sound. We stiffened and sensed in each other that we knew something, or someone was down there on the beach. We continued very still not a movement between us as we watched the beach.

"There," I pointed. "I just saw a bit of a light. I would swear it was someone's watch. We had better call it in and report it."

"Bollocks to that," said Franky, slowly climbing over the banking and sliding down the other side.

I felt Micky move to my right and follow Franky over the top. I looked around, couldn't see anyone else so shrugged and followed them over the top. We inched down through the sand dunes and grasses towards the edge of the beach. It was then we heard voices and they weren't English ones either. Bloody hell, I thought, here we go the bloody Nazi's have turned up after all. Was it a full-blown invasion or a few chancers trying to sneak in.

As we watched, it looked like four guys dressed in black, pulling a dingy onto the beach. This was some bloody Nazi spies but unfortunately for them, they tried the wrong bloody beach. What do we do now though, my adrenaline was absolutely buzzing? Should we just shoot first and ask questions later; surely no one would question that approach.

As they came near to us, Franky jumped up and shouted, "Who goes there?" It made me jump a mile in the darkness and it certainly rattled the four guys who started shouting.

Micky was up and on to them like a flash. He whacked the nearest guy with the butt of his rifle and he went down and out straight away. One of the guys leapt at him shouting "no, no," but Micky wasn't listening to that; he turned and was grappling with the guy. He overpowered him, Micky overpowered most guys in a fight and started giving him a right good hiding. The other two guys raised their hands and I covered them with my rifle. There were saying, "Don't shoot, don't shoot, it's exercise," in broken English with a definite foreign twang.

"Shut up," I said. "Franky, what do we do now?"

"Let's get them back to the shed. We can tie them up in there and go and get help. Try and find out who the hell they are and what they are up to," he said.

Micky dragged the two guys to their feet who he had inflicted some pain on. I picked up his rifle and we marched them off the beach with our rifles right in their backs. They seemed a bit subdued now which is just the way I liked it. Where we had our observation post, we had a bit of a shed where we stored stuff and could brew up. We pushed them in there and Franky tied up their hands and sat them on the floor. The two Micky had dealt with were not with it at all.

"Right, me and Micky will keep our eye on these bastards while you go and get the boss, Franky," I said.

"I'm on it," he said and took off.

It must have been ten minutes before he returned with Captain Smart and the sarge.

"What's going on here, Mulligan?" he said.

"Caught these guys sneaking out of the water, Cap," I said and opened the door.

The captain flashed his torch inside, and we saw the four guys closely for the first time.

"You stupid sod," said the Captain. "This is the polish team on exercises tonight, testing our readiness for defence. You were in the briefing. You were supposed to capture them and raise the alarm. Two of them look like they have had a right beating. Is this your doing, Mulligan?"

"What briefing, sir, no one told us they were testing us out," I said defensively.

"For Christ sake, Mulligan," said the sarge. "We briefed all the unit at roll call tonight before we set off out for the night patrols."

"Ah, we missed that briefing, Sarge," I said, noticing my two buddies were keeping too bloody quiet and I seemed to be copping all the grief. "We had to go down the depot if you remember for additional ammunition."

"Jesus, Mulligan and you didn't think to ask what the briefing was about? All right," said the Captain, "get these two guys some medical treatment back at base and get those ropes off the other two and I want to see the three of you in my office first thing. Understood!"

"Yes sir," we all mumbled as he stomped off.

Chapter 11

The next morning, over breakfast, we were all a bit miffed as it seemed we would be getting a kicking for the activities the night before.

"As I see it," said Micky. "I reckon we did a cracking job last night. They were trying to test our observation skills and test our alertness. Well, I say we reacted bloody well which just shows you lads no one was getting by us."

"Yeah I get that," said Franky. "And I reckon they might have been pinning hero medals on us if you hadn't given those two lads a good hiding! Same old bloody Micky."

"I will clock you in a minute, Frank," said Micky, getting up from the table.

"All right, you two. I agree I think we did a good job. We just need to lay it on thick, you know, it was pitch black, they didn't respond correctly to our challenge and they weren't speaking bloody English. If you ask me, it's their own fault sneaking about, got what they deserved!" I said.

"Come on then, let's go and see what the cap has to say," said Micky, "but I think we should leave the talking to you, Vic, you have the gift of the gab."

"Oh, cheers for that," I said. "Just what I need in the bloody line of fire. OK, I will take the lead then, you two back me up and keep your mouths shut if you can."

We marched on down to the office and I knocked on the door. There was no answer, so I waited what seemed like ten minutes and then knocked again. The door flew open and it was Sergeant Windle. "All right, Mulligan, we know you are here, no need to keep knocking the door down," he said.

I thought oh Christ that's not a great start and we marched in and saluted the cap who was set behind his desk.

"All right, you three, stand at ease," he said as the sarge closed the door behind us. "Between you and me, I thought you lads did a pretty good job last night. Good to see you were alert and not slacking off and good to see you have a bit of grit about you to tackle that boat crew on your own. However, you know if you see anything suspicious, you should call it in, and you didn't. No room for heroics in my team. Say it was the Nazis landing, you could have blown a hole right in our defences if they had overpowered you."

"No chance of that, Captain," said Micky, leaning forward with a big grin on his face.

"Yes, maybe that's the case, O'Flaherty, but still you didn't follow process and for that, I should kick your arses.

Also, you injured two colleagues from the local Polish Brigade, and we have a good bit of bridge building to do there. Not only that, the guy you beat up on was there senior officer Captain Kowalczyk and having just come from breakfast with him, he doesn't look too great. Fortunately for you, I think I have smoothed it over by promising I will deal with you accordingly."

"That's not fair, Captain," I said. "We didn't know he was a captain and they didn't exactly try and explain what they were doing sneaking about on a beach. I would do the same again if I was in that situation."

"No, you wouldn't, Mulligan. You would have sent a runner back to HQ and report what you had seen and let myself or Sargent Windle come down and make the decisions before acting, wouldn't you, Mulligan?" he said sarcastically.

"Yes sir," I said sheepishly.

"Look, I know sitting around here isn't doing any of us any good and we are all itching to get into the action. So, tensions are high, and I can, therefore, understand what happened. The good news is we are not going to be here much longer. The threat of invasion has well and truly passed and the powers that be are disbanding the Dorset's in a month or so."

"That's good news, sir?" I asked.

"It is, Mulligan, as we are being transferred to a new brigade of the 1st Infantry division. However, in the New

Year, they are forming a new 38th (Irish) Infantry Brigade and I think I have done my share of baby-sitting you three, so I am transferring you across there early while they get themselves established."

"We will miss you, Captain," I said. "Will it more playing soldiers in England, do you know?"

"I believe, gentlemen," he said, standing up from his desk and for the first time, smiling, "that your immediate futures lie in North Africa!"

Theatre of War – North Africa 1942

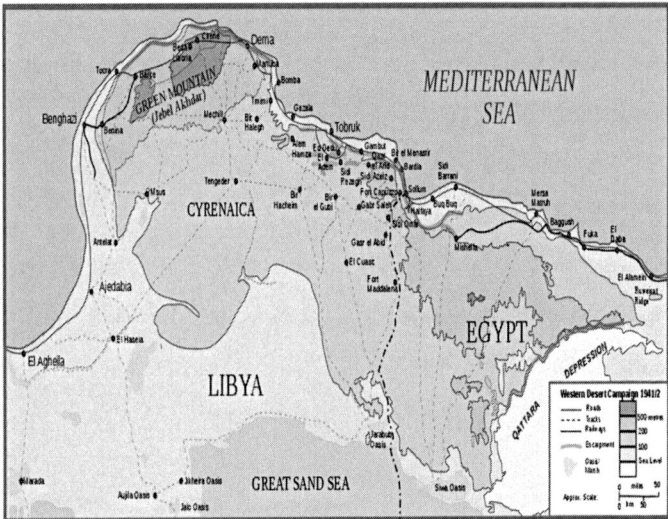

Map source

https://en.wikipedia.org/wiki/Second_Battle_of_El_Alam
ein

Chapter 12

Egypt September 1942

We had to look up Egypt on a map we found of the world. Obviously, I had heard of Africa but had no idea what to expect. I thought there would be lions running around and how would that work with tanks and infantry? But what I did know was that was where all the fighting was going on now and therefore, that's where we wanted to be. We had left the charming Captain Smart and hooked up with a New Zealand unit who were flying out to Egypt in the next few months. That gave us time to train and keep our fitness going with the New Zealand lads. The plan was to hitch a ride with these guys and then find our new unit when we got there. Unbelievably, we found out later that we got into Africa a few months before the rest of the Irish Brigade and were in the wrong country altogether!

The New Zealand captain was happy to have us along and was one heck of an excited guy. He explained to us that they were reinforcements flying out to join the other brigades over there on the eve of, what he called, the biggest battle of the war so far. Forget the Battle of France and Britain, he said this was the big one. The idea was to turn the tide and shove the Germans and Italians out of Africa and from there, form a base to win the war. Sounded great to me and sounded like we would get to meet the enemy at last. I couldn't help feeling that the war had been raging for over two years and I hadn't done anything yet. Now was our time.

Once we landed in Egypt, we were transported to a place called El Alamein. Preparations for the big push across North Africa, the captain referred too, seemed well underway. You could literally touch the excitement.

It was absolute chaos. The noise was incredible as what seemed like hundreds of massive guns were firing shell after shell over our heads towards the enemy. The big push must have started but no one had told us! There were literally thousands of troops, tanks and vehicles everywhere. I had heard that the Brits has been building up an army from all over the world, but this just took your breath away. I just couldn't believe it. My experience before this were a few platoons together in training and I had seen a few mechanised vehicles in England, but this was incredible. I couldn't wait to be part of it. Honestly, I think it was the most exciting moment of my entire life.

I tracked down the New Zealand captain and tried to explain that we needed to find our brigade to hook up with them and get ourselves into this war. "There is absolutely no chance, Mulligan," he said. "Everything is currently geared to push forward straight at the enemy and as you can hear, the guns have already opened up. I can use you so stick with us as we are moving out first thing into the line and will be engaging the enemy tomorrow." He broke off as one of his sergeants handed him some orders. He read them and spoke to his sergeant who jogged off to start organising the platoon.

"So, Captain, we stick with you guys for now and join in the fight tomorrow, yes?" I said.

"Yeah, Mulligan, that's your best option. Report to Sergeant James and tell him I told you guys to join his platoon and take his orders from there."

I went back to join the guys. "Captain says there is no way we can find our unit in this lot. The plan is to stick with the New Zealanders and get stuck into the fighting tomorrow when they move out," I said.

"That will do for me. World War Two, here come the Dublin lads," said Franky.

"About bloody time," said Micky.

We collected our kit and went off to meet the sarge. He pointed us to a temporary tent for the night while the big boys planned out what we were going to do in the morning. He told us to get some food and then try and get some sleep. I looked at him as though he was mad as I could hardly hear him over the sound of the guns. I wasn't sure how we were going to get any sleep in this lot and with my excitement in overdrive. Looking back now, there was never any fear or thoughts about what could go wrong which is incredible to comprehend. We just wanted to join in and feel like we were finally part of a war that had been going on for years without us.

I did get some sleep that night. I don't know what time, but I definitely nodded off for a few hours. I woke up on a regular basis as I shifted on my mattress and every time was met with the noise of guns and a war going on outside the tent. It must have been around six am when the platoon was stood to arms if you like and we all gathered around the trucks outside which would transport us to the front. The sarge came around and told us to get some breakfast from the mess tent and then gather back together in thirty minutes to go through a last check of our kit, weapons and ammunition. We wandered off to the mess tent.

"I am not sure I am that hungry," said Frank. "My stomach feels as tight as a drum. Just want to get on with it now."

"Well, I could eat a horse," said Micky and I had to agree with him.

We loaded up our plates with as much as they would let us have and tucked in. My thinking was who knows what lies out there and when we would see a mess tent again. We finished up and gathered round our designated vehicle with the rest of the guys. The sarge took us through the process of what kit we needed for a few days out there in the desert.

We were all allocated ammunition and checked through the rifle mechanisms to make sure they were in good order. I remembered the training and the message that you didn't get a second chance in battle if your gun didn't work. Everyone helped check everyone else's kit and you could feel a mixture of excitement and nerves. Some of the guys looked horrified, others seemed blasé about it all and sat back relaxed with a smoke.

The sarge came up to the squad, "Men, stand down but keep at the ready. There is a load of confusion about when we move out so I will stick with the captain until we get the orders to move. I will let you know what's happening shortly."

There was an audible groan from the guys, and we all dropped our kit where we were and sat down to relax. Everyone broke open the smokes and tried to relax as best we could. We must have sat around most of the day with the sounds of the battle a few miles ahead of us. As I sat there, I realised how used to the shells and aircraft buzzing overhead I had become, moving from the safety of our lines to release hell on the enemy. I spent some time just watching the skies and thought surely, they must be knocking the stuffing out of them.

It was early afternoon when the sarge came back. "Right, mount up we are moving out. We have the pleasure of pushing on through the minefield and engaging the enemy head on. The idea is we blaze a path through so that the engineers can clear the minefields behind us and allow our tanks to come rolling through and flatten the Jerrys," he said.

He must have seen the startled expressions on our faces to this terrific news. "Don't panic," he said. "It's an anti-tank minefield and, therefore, no threat to us simple infantry but our tanks can't get through unless we clear the way. The lorries will take us so far and then we are on our own. As you can see, we have loads of air and artillery support. Who knows when we get there, maybe the enemy will have had enough? Mount up!" he shouted.

We clambered on board and then set off in convoy. I don't know how many trucks, but I couldn't see the back of the line as I stared out the back of the truck. It was a bumpy ride and I couldn't tell you how long it lasted before the trucks slammed to a halt. You could hear the sergeants and captains dishing out the orders and rallying the troops together. This was it we were going to war.

"Good luck, you two," I said, looking at what felt like the two most important people in all the world to me at that time. They gave me rueful grins and we jumped out of the truck and moved around following the platoon.

Chapter 13

We formed up and moved out. Hundreds of men loaded up moving out towards the enemy. Slightly walking slightly jogging along. No one was shooting at us which felt bizarre, so we just kept on going. I have no idea how far we covered but it must have been a few miles before the enemy opened up on us. Believe me, it's nothing like the movies, everyone dived for cover and kept their heads down. This was the first time anyone had shot at me and I suddenly thought they are trying to kill me. There was lots of cover with holes in the sand from shells I guess, and everyone made for them and started firing back like mad at the enemy. I could make out where they were about a hundred yards or so ahead.

The sarge climbed up and dashed forward picking out more cover and we all followed him. I saw my first person get it. One of the blokes from the platoon to my right was hit two or three times and went down in the sand. It was impossible to see if I hit anyone with my shooting, but I like to think I was doing the right thing. All the time our friends in the sky were darting over us and giving the enemy some treatment. We kept moving forward and felt like we were making headway. Impossible to know if we were winning but if we were going forward, we must be doing alright.

It was absolutely boiling, and the sweat was just running down my face. I was so parched but there was no time for a drink. The adrenalin just kept pushing us forward. It started to go dark around the battle. One thing I had noticed since arriving in Egypt was how quick the sun went down. Once the heat went out of it, it simply dropped out of the sky. The darker it went, the less the firing was from both sides. The message came along the lines to dig in and reinforce for the night. The first thing I did was take a big slug of water and check on my two buddies.

I looked around the hole we were in. Somehow the three of us had stuck together and appeared to be in one piece. There were four other blokes in our den, and we started shovelling sand up on the rampart to give us more cover.

"You OK, Franky," I said.

"Yeah, mate, I am all right. Absolutely knackered but other than that, nothing's missing. So many of the blokes didn't make it though, seen loads of them drop," he said.

"Yeah, so did I. That was a few hours of your life you wouldn't want to repeat," I said as we kept on shovelling.

Micky slid down next to us and took out his water bottle taking a massive swig before saying, "Wow, that was amazing, have you ever seen anything like that?"

"No, just thank God, we all got through it," I said. We all sat back and took a bit of time to gather ourselves. Suddenly, a burst of fire came over to our left and the blokes there started firing back. We scrambled to our feet and looked out, but I couldn't see a bloody thing. There were flashes coming from the enemy, so we opened up firing off a few rounds before it all died down again.

I felt exhausted now and slid back down and started rummaging in my rucksack for something to eat. The blokes did the same and nobody said anything for some time as we ate our rations. We were knackered as Franky had said and slumped where we were. The sarge appeared and jumped into our hole. "Well done, boys. You need to try and get some sleep now. We will get a rest bite until first light so make the most of it. Post a guard while the others get some rest. It's going to start getting light about six o'clock, and then we are back on the move. We haven't cleared the minefield yet and our tanks are still relying on us getting through to the other side."

"OK, Sarge," I said. "I'll do first stint; Franky, I will wake you in two hours."

"All right, Vic, cheers, mate," he said.

I perched myself at the top of the barricade we had built up, looking out into no man's land. It was pitch dark now so nothing really to see but at least the temperature had dropped to a nice level. I sat there still as an owl waiting to dive on its prey. You could hear the sounds of war all around to the south and the north but in our sector, all seemed to be calm. What a day that was. I had spent so long wanting to get involved and now I had I realised just how horrific it had been. We had lost loads of guys and I don't mind admitting I started to fill up and had a little weep, there all alone in the dark in a desert in North Africa facing an army out there somewhere. Wow, what a change that was from the dockyards of Dublin and I thought of Ma and how she was doing. I hadn't really been writing home and made a promise to do so if I got out of this one alive.

Chapter 14

I woke Franky a couple of hours in and we swapped places. I curled up in the bottom of the den and was asleep in seconds. Movement of men around me stirred me first thing. It wasn't quite light, but you could see the first indications of dawn on the horizon. We all started to stretch and yawn and break out the rations before the order, we knew would come to attack.

About twenty minutes later, the guns started up again. You heard the bangs and the woosh overhead as they headed out towards the enemy and then the huge explosions when they landed. We jumped to the ready and just hoped those explosions were doing some serious damage. We held firm for what felt like ages before the order went up to attack and we went berserk, firing as much as we could, hoping to swamp the opposition. We kept moving, firing and ducking and again the trend through the day was a forward one. We must be doing OK surely, I remember thinking.

It was about mid-afternoon when we started to come under serious heavy firepower. Far more than we had seen so far. The word amongst the lads was that it was a hard line of dug in tanks, 88mm flak guns and anti-tank weaponry and it was targeted right on top of us. There was no way we could get any further and we became bogged down. Just as it was looking bleak, we saw the cavalry coming up behind us. Hundreds of tanks came past us and started opening up on the line. We all started cheering as one hell of a battle started. I guess we had cleared the minefield and now our role changed to backing up the tanks and moving up with them.

The heat was intensive again and I was literally wet through with sweat. I looked around and there was smoke everywhere. Burning tanks and vehicles were strewn all over the desert all around us but also smoke was everywhere on the horizons wherever you looked. It was just carnage! I also noticed a terrible stench and put that down to the hundreds of dead bodies you could see lying out in the open. Nothing we could do for those guys now. The medics were working overtime on the injured and we all helped getting blokes back from the line and into the relative safety of the waiting ambulances.

It was difficult to know how it was going but we managed to edge forward before dusk arrived and we started to dig in again. Was the battle going to plan we had no idea but as I understood, it our job was to clear the mines and get our tanks into the fight and that had certainly happened.

The next day and night continued with the same theme we had already seen. The tanks and artillery battling with the enemy's tanks and big guns and every now and again, we edged forward. On the morning of the fourth day, we were withdrawn from the front and replaced with a fresh contingent from the free French Army we were told. God knows what they must have thought of us as we passed in the desert. All our faces were literally caked in sand and dust and our clothes were filthy and covered in blood. Luckily for me, the blood wasn't mine although it was that of my friends' and buddies' from the platoon. At this point though, there was just no time to dwell on that.

We were picked up in trucks and transported back to a base camp out of the range of the big guns. The first thing we all did was dive in the showers and clean ourselves up. After a shave and something to eat, we almost started feeling human again. We found a bunk in one of the tents and crashed out into a deep sleep extremely exhausted but all three of us alive and in one piece.

Chapter 15

We were told straight away the next day that this would just be a couple of days to recuperate from the sharp end of the battle. Everything was being thrown at the enemy and there just wasn't the men and machines to sit it out for too long. That was OK with us, we could make two or three days feel like a lifetime just then. The captain told everyone how proud he was of the fight we had put up over the last three days. We had indeed achieved our objective of getting the tanks into the action and although he couldn't tell us exactly what was happening or even if it was going well, he was well pleased with us.

This optimism though had to be checked by the amount of faces that just weren't around anymore and had been lost and left out on that battlefield. I sat there for hours contemplating this and just really thanked the fates that I had come out of it so far unscathed. Remarkably, so had Franky and Micky and they still had that determined steely-eyed expression about them that told me they would be right there with me when we went back in.

It was incredible to think that three or four days ago, we were all novices to the horrors of battle and war but how quickly we had come to terms with it and knuckled down to fight and accept your own fate. You gained a lot out there in the heat of battle, but you also lost something. Something about being human and understanding how precious life was. You somehow didn't care too much about yourself but absolutely would do anything for your buddies. It also didn't seem to bother you – well, me anyway and I guess the rest of the lads – that all the shots we were firing off were probably killing other humans across on the enemy lines. In fact, thinking about it afterwards, every time we moved up, we passed literally hundreds of dead German and Italian bodies.

The changes I felt in myself and the rest of the platoon became obvious when later in the afternoon of that first day away from the line, the platoon received five new replacement recruits. You could see them wincing at the sounds of the guns and the battle, whereas now we just didn't seem to notice them. We made them feel welcome and were grateful to have them on board. After all, that was us just a few days ago. We were buddied up with the recruits to give them a helping hand and the benefit of our experience through the next few days of preparation for battle. The sarge came over. "Mulligan," he said, "this is Private Taylor just in from England. Can you show him the ropes and stick with him when we go back into the line?"

"Sure thing, Sarge," I said while extending a handshake with Taylor. "Everyone knows me as Vic." The Sarge marched off.

"That doesn't sound much like a Kiwi accent, mate," he said.

"No," I said laughing, "it's a long story, Me, Franky there and big Micky," they mock saluted Taylor as I mentioned their names, "are from Dublin. We got mixed up with the Kiwi lot when we arrived and haven't been able to get back to where we belong. Anyhow this feels like home now," I said, gesturing to the camp around us.

"That's good with me," said Taylor. "We're all on the same side. As I heard it, there is every nationality you can think of in this skirmish. Is it always as noisy and chaotic as this?"

"You ain't seen nothing yet, mate, wait while we move back up to the front. You can't hear yourself think. So, what do we call you?"

Taylor shrugged. "My first name is Finn."

"Finn! Never heard of it," said Franky. "The only Finn I have ever heard of is Huckleberry Finn. A book I read when I was a kid. We'll call you Huckleberry or Huck for short."

"All right, I can live with that," said the newly christened Huckleberry.

So, Finn Taylor became Huck to his new mates in the platoon.

We wandered off to give Huck his first taste of the food in the mess tent. While we were eating, I remembered my promise to myself on the battlefield to write home so when we got back, I cadged some paper, pencil and envelop and took myself off to a quiet corner. What to write? I couldn't tell them about how bad it really was so would have to paint a different picture:

Hello Ma,

Sorry I have written in a while but have been on the move. Last time I said we were leaving England, but I didn't know where we were going. You'll never believe it, but we ended up in Egypt of all places. Can you imagine a Mulligan in North Africa Ma! That's something to tell everyone back home.

Anyhow I am fine. We have finally seen a bit of action with the enemy, but all is going well. I'm currently enjoying a few rest days out of the fight and enjoying playing cards with the blokes. Micky and Franky are also doing well.

It's so hot here compared to Dublin at this time of the year, so I am having to keep ducking out of the sun where I can. You know me never was one for sunbathing.

I hope everyone is Ok back there, please give them all my love. Write back and let me know what's happening back in good old Dublin – it's a different world than here!

OK Ma take care of yourself. I will write again next week.
All my Love, Vic

We got three days' rest and recovery in the end where I seemed to do nothing more than eat and sleep. The heat was too hot for me so I would cover in the shade all day long but some of the blokes would lie out there working on their tan. When word finally came that we were going back in, we heard it was an operation called Supercharge. Sounded good to us so we pulled out kit together, replenished the ammunition and stocked up on rations. The four of us, as we now were with the addition of Huck, ambled over to the trucks ready to go.

Chapter 16

This time the tactics seemed different. It appeared we would be attacking and clearing a path through the minefields again for the tanks but this time, we were setting out in the dark! It was late evening as the trucks rolled us forward to the start line. The heavy guns had been pounding away for hours and the enemy's front line was getting hit hard. We heard loads of planes overhead but couldn't make them out in the dark night sky but as we neared the battle, there were many fires lighting up the battlefield.

We dismounted and set out and seemed to make steady progress. The fighting didn't seem as intense as last time and we seemed to make loads of distance before being told to dig in as the sun started to rise. Loads of armoured vehicles passed us and darted out into no man's land. We watched as they threw themselves onto the guns of the opposition. It really was ferocious and no place for us infantry blokes. We held our position while the main battle happened in front of us. Tank after tank seemed to be destroyed but in turn the enemy seemed to be copping for a right battering. This went on all day, but our tanks just couldn't break through. Towards early evening, we began attacking again and moving forward.

We used the same tactics as the previous battle that proved successful: using the armoured vehicles as cover and moving up to the cover of the bomb craters all the time engaging the enemy. This went on for a couple of days when we finally seemed to break through the enemy gun positions. There were heavy guns destroyed and littered everywhere but we didn't stop which surprised me. We were urged on and continued the attack.

In the darkening evening of the third or fourth day, I can't be sure, we dived for cover in a crater as out in front of us enemy tanks appeared and drove straight for us on both sides and carried on passed. I must admit I began to panic and yelled at Franky, "I think we have come to bloody far. Looks like we might have crossed their lines."

"Jesus, that's not good; we are sitting ducks out here, Vic," he said.

"Keep your eyes peeled forward everyone in case their infantry comes through," I shouted. "I can see movement out there." We formed up in a defensive position and carried on firing out in front while tank skirmishes were going on behind us. We really were hung out to dry here but we just had to try and keep calm. A couple of explosions landed very close by and stunned my senses. When I pulled myself together and started firing back, I could hear screaming behind me and saw Huck had taken a hit. "Huck's hit, cover me while I try and help him," I said to Micky.

I jumped back down to Huck. He was covered in blood and screaming. I fished in my bag and dug out some morphine jabs and hit him with them. I had some basic medical equipment like bandages, medicine and swabs and looked him over. Looked like his right forearm had taken a hit of shrapnel and was a bit of a mess but his right leg had taken a hit and was bleeding quite badly.

"Hang in there, mate," I said as the morphine started to quiet Huck down a bit. There was a lot of blood just above the knee. I knew I had to stop it and started to rig up a tunica on his thigh. The shooting in the background had stopped and Micky appeared next to me.

"How is he, is it bad?" he said.

"He's took a hit to his arm and leg. I need to stop the bleeding in his leg. Here, hold this bandage in place while I tighten it."

Between us, we patched him up and the blood loss eased off. He was well out of it now with the morphine though.

"What's happening out there, why's the firing stopped?" I said.

"We can't see anything, Vic, reckon they have dug in for the night as well."

"We got to get Huck out of here and back to the medics," I said. "We have a real problem though. If we are behind enemy lines, then we have had it, mate; no one will be looking for us. As I see it, we must sneak back while its dark, but I reckon it must be a few hundred yards and we are going to have to drag him all the way. It also looks like the tanks are still at it so we can't go strolling through that lot either."

"Let's keep our heads down for a bit and see how it plays out, Vic."

"All right, Micky, sounds like a plan but we can't wait too long with the state Huck is in."

We sat tight for about thirty minutes and everything seemed to calm down. Even the tanks seemed to have given up the fight. There were plenty of them on fire so maybe they had just blown each other to bits and there were none left! There were four other guys as well as the four of us. I gathered them together and whispered, "Looks like the battle is done for now. We must get ourselves back to the rest of the lads while it's still dark. Huck's in a bad way, so we will have to drag him with us."

"I'll carry him," said Micky.

"You sure, it won't be easy?"

"He is only a strip of a lad. I reckon I could carry him a few hundred yards, Vic."

"OK then, let's pull out. We need to move quietly but smartly covering our front and back. We are as likely to get shot by our own lads as we approach them, so we need to be awake," I said.

We stripped as much kit off Huck as we could, and Micky lifted him over his shoulder like a fireman's lift. Huck grumbled so he was still alive, and we set out. We jogged in a crouched position and thankfully found no one was shooting at us. We covered a few hundred yards and passed a couple of burning tanks. I couldn't make out if they were ours or theirs.

Micky dropped to his knees "Sorry lads, I can't carry him any further."

"That's all right, mate, it's great you got this far," I said "Franky, grab his collar and shoulder and we will drag him between us. This slowed us down big time, but we couldn't be far from the rest of the boys. We carried on like this for twenty minutes when a shout went out 'who goes there?'"

"It's all right," we all shouted. "Friendlies coming back in with an injured man."

Thankfully, they shouted before shooting and not the other way around. We were met by a group of lads who took Huck off us on a stretcher and whisked him away. That was it, he was gone, we didn't see where he went and I just had to hope he would make it.

We made our way through the ranks of men and met with a captain who told us to carry on back through to the trucks. He said we looked like we had had enough of a beating in this battle for anyone and time to get ourselves out of there. We weren't going to argue with that. It was such a relief climbing on that truck I can tell you. We were very subdued as the truck rumbled away, but somehow, we had escaped death again. All we could do now was pray for Huck's survival.

Chapter 17

We ended up back in the reserve area and joined the rest of our platoon that had been pulled out apparently the day before we did, but they had given us up as dead when we didn't show up. We crashed out for a few hours before the captain came to see us.

"You blokes look like you're in a right state," he said.

"Jesus, Cap, thanks for that vote of confidence," Franky said.

"That was a really tough few days lads but were winning and the bastards are on the retreat. You did a heck of a job getting that young lad out of there."

"Huck, how is he, Cap, he didn't look to good last night?" I said.

"Huck? Do you mean young Taylor? Yes, he is still alive and has been evacuated out back to blighty. Fingers crossed he pulls through."

"Bloody hope so, Cap, he was such a brave kid out there," I said.

"OK." He paused thoughtfully. "We have been given orders to sit tight for a few days so spend the time getting some sleep and getting yourselves back on your feet. We then need to look at getting you back to the Irish lot where you belong. I will make some enquiries," he said as he stood up and left our tent.

"Cheers, Cap," I said.

"Good news on young Huckleberry then, let's hope he pulls through and gets out of this hell once and for all. Think he's done his bit," said Micky.

With that, we all crashed out again.

We spent three days with our feet up with the sounds of battle off in the far distance which is where I was getting to like it. The sarge popped his head in our tent and said that the captain wanted to see us. Hopefully, he had found out where we should be and was sending us off to join our Irish buddies who we hadn't even seen yet, since being in Egypt. We pulled ourselves together and marched off to the captain's office/tent.

"Hey there, boys," he said as we stood to attention and saluted. "At ease. You have been sulking around here long enough, so I have a mission for the three of you."

"Did you find the Irish boys, Captain?" said Micky.

"No, I haven't had chance yet, O'Flaherty, but you can't sit around here all the time looking sorry for yourselves. So, let's put you to some use." He stood up and took us across to a map on the side of the tent wall. He used his stick to point to the map. "This is where we currently are, and this is where the final elements of the battle is lingering but we have them beat and they are falling back."

"Good news, sir, kicked them out of Egypt altogether," I said.

"Quite, Mulligan, this is the turning point of the whole war and you boys played your part. Anyhow, see this dark area here on the map?" he said banging the map with his stick on a shaded area. "This is the Quattara Depression and the southern flank of the battlefield. It's believed to be impassable to tanks and heavy armour so that's concentrated the battle in this area near the coast. However, now the rascals are on the retreat, it would just like them to try and attack our flank back through here. We are putting together small teams to go out there and scout the place just to make sure it's clear and I want you to form one of these teams and take a jeep out there. Two to three days maximum to make your way a hundred miles or so in and back."

"Sounds easy enough, Cap. What do we do if we find anything out there?" I said.

"Report what you find, Mulligan, so we can assess the situation and decide what to do. You move out first thing tomorrow. The jeeps have been loaded with all the equipment you need. Any questions?"

"No sir," we said.

"OK, good luck and no heroics," he saluted us as we turned and left.

We went back to the tent and started to gather our kit together.

"This sounds a simple one, Vic. Drive round the desert and have a little picnic or two out there and drive back," said Franky.

"It does, Franky, unless of course we do meet a few tanks out there and that could really spoil our little trip," I replied.

"As I heard it, mate, no heroics. If we see anything, we call it in and leg it back here. Easy!" he said.

"We'll see, boys, but it definitely beats sitting around here. Sounds like a bit of a lark!"

We had a few good beers that night and a hearty sleep before the sarge woke us just before sunup. We had checked over the jeep the evening before and it looked up to the job. The captain was right, it was loaded with supplies and the important radio which would be our lifeline out there. After breakfast, we set off out into the desert with our map and planned route they had instructed us to take.

Chapter 18

As we set out, the going was good while we were still in the desert, but it soon became obvious once we hit the depression. Going was heavy and we literally dropped to 20 miles an hour or less. The place was a baron area full of salt pans, sand dunes and salt marches so we were glad we were in the jeep that was built for this type of terrain.

Our brief was to keep moving out on a 210-degree heading cutting southwest across the depression for two days or until we felt we were out of the other side. We were to make notes and report back to the captain using the radio each evening on anything we saw including fly overs by both our and the enemy's planes. The men in charge of the army were interested in what was going on in this area, probably to reassure themselves that it was OK to push on along the coast and weren't going to get any nasty surprises in the rear.

The first day was very uneventful. We saw a few planes and our brief was try not to get spotted! We thought this was a bloody stupid request as we were out in the open although now and again, we did come across sand dunes that gave a bit of cover from the horizon.

The second day though was not so uneventful! We were making decent progress and had decided we would go as far as we could that day, then bed down for the night and then turn around and make the two-day return trip back to base. We were travelling by a series of sand banks to our right for a few miles when we were spotted by a plane overhead. Franky made a note of it in the notebook to report back later when it started banking around and lowering its flight towards us.

"Shit, lads, this plane looks like it wants a piece of us," said Micky in the back.

I was driving. "I will get in tight to the sand dunes over there and, hopefully, they just fly over us. They will be getting data just as we are," I said.

"Well, let's hope he's not board and trigger happy then," said Micky, "as he is heading straight for us."

The plane buzzed overhead not much more than 50 feet at a guess and flew off over the dunes. We were in them now, so I stopped the engine and we climbed out watching the plane which unfortunately, started to bank right and level off coming back towards us, looking like it had a purpose. We moved to the other side of the jeep as it approached. To our amazement, it started firing with its machine guns and we dived for cover under the jeep. The jeep took several hits and one of the spare oil cans burst into flames as the plane took off into the distance.

We jumped up. "Everyone OK?" I said. "I bet he only had enough fuel for one flyby."

"Get the fire out, Micky," said Franky. Micky was grappling with the fire extinguisher and got to work on the back of the jeep and had the fire out until it just smoked. We looked at the back of the jeep which was a bit charred where most of our supplies were and the bloody radio which had had it. Looking around the rest of the jeep, there was a bit of damage, but it didn't look too bad.

"Front tyre's punctured, lads," said Franky. "Good job we have a replacement, should be able to get that switched over easy enough."

"That's the least of our problems," I said. Looking under the jeep, there was loads of petrol pouring out of the tank. "It must have a bloody bullet hole in the petrol tank. We need to catch it in something." But there wasn't anything that wasn't fire damaged on the back of the jeep and we watched that precious liquid drain into the sand until it was empty.

"Well, that's literally put a hole in our trip, and we have no spare petrol," said Micky.

"Yeah, we are in a bit of trouble here, boys," I said. "We have the water flasks and some rations in the front of the jeep, so we are OK with that for a few days, but we are miles from anywhere. Can't really tell how far we have come but looks to me like we are out of the depression so that's at least eighty to a hundred miles walk back – that's a heck of a challenge."

"Well, we can't do anything now. Let's make camp for the night, have something to eat and a good night's sleep and we can get up early while the temperature is still reasonably cool and make a dent in that walk. You never know we maybe missed when we don't report in and they may come looking for us," said Franky.

"Bet they don't, Franky," I said. "I don't want to be all doom and gloom, but they have more to worry about than three blokes out here."

"Did anyone see if it was one of ours or one of theirs," said Micky. "I will be totally cheesed off if it was one of our own blokes that shot us up."

"Couldn't see, mate, as it came out of the sun, but it doesn't matter who the hell it was, they did the job," I said.

Chapter 19

We made camp and broke out the mini stoves to get a brew on and something to eat. Afterwards, I climbed the dune we were sheltering on and sat atop of it looking out to the horizons in all directions. Nothing to see but it was a heck of a view. After about an hour, Franky scrambled up to join me.

"What you doing up here then, mate? Micky's asleep," he said.

"Just chilling out and enjoying the view. It will get dark soon and I have always found the desert a bit creepy in the dark."

Franky was looking out at the view when he said, "There's something coming in the distance, mate, I am sure of it. Did you miss that?" he said shielding his eyes and looking in the direction we were heading. I looked across and there was the tell tail sign of a dust cloud in the air a few miles south, hugging the other side of the sand dunes we had been using as cover.

"Bloody hell, Franky, you are right. Missed that completely but then again, I wasn't expecting anything out here. Wonder if they know we are here from that plane attack earlier and I wonder if they are friendlies. I'm going to get the binoculars for a better look."

I was back in a minute and trained the binocs on the approaching vehicle. I couldn't quite make it out, but it was moving steady, so I guessed it had to be a jeep of some kind probably scouting out the depression as we had been doing. My worry was it was coming from the wrong direction and heading for the coast probably on their side of the lines.

"Go wake Micky, Franky, and break out the weapons, I can't believe that's one of ours coming from that direction. I'll keep eyes on."

The lads were back in about five minutes with the rifles, machine guns and grenades and lay down on the top of the dune next to me. We all had the binocs on the vehicle now and could make out a small people carrier with three or four blokes in it. It had the grey appearance of an enemy vehicle.

"I am pretty sure that's Jerry," I said. "What do we do keep our heads down and hope they go by or give them hell, steel their ride and leg it back to base?"

"I say we kick their arse," said Micky.

"So do I," said Franky. "I would rather have a shootout and hope to nick their ride, anything rather than that bloody long walk back to safety."

"OK, I'll have a bit of that, but we need to get into a better ambush position than this." We slid down the dune and dug ourselves in at the bottom.

"They won't see us here," said Micky. "But we need to take the driver out first to bring the vehicle to a stop. If I go up the dune a bit and hide myself there with the rifle, I will take the shot. Better shot than you two anyway."

"All right, I like that. You take the first shot and once we hear that, we will open up. If we don't get them all straightaway, we can use the grenades but that's not going to do the vehicle any good. You need to let them come in pretty close though, Micky, as our only chance is the first minute or so of the surprise."

The vehicle kept on coming and was only a few hundred yards away now. I could see four blokes in it, two front and two back. They wouldn't be expecting a ground attack, possibly one from the air which is why I guessed they were hugging the side of the dune not to stand out on the horizon. Two hundred yards now and we could see it all quite clearly. I was looking at that running vehicle with envious eyes I can tell you.

A hundred yards and getting less by the second. A shot rang out and the front windscreen shattered, and the car careered left and right. Impossible to see if Micky had nailed the driver so we just opened up with everything we had, pouring bullets into the vehicle which ground to a stop sideways about forty yards ahead. After that burst, we ceased fire as Micky joined us.

"Did we get them?" he said.

There was smoke and not much movement. We edged out of our cover and started to make our way across no man's land. We could clearly see two people in the car, and they looked dead or certainly dying. As confidence rose, shots started to ring out and we dived for cover. Someone was alive in there! We fanned out to try and pin them down and returned fire. This went on for maybe ten minutes. A stalemate really with each keeping the other at arm's length. Was it one or two guys, I couldn't make it out? Just as I was trying to work it out, there were two explosions at the jeep about three seconds apart and Micky charged out from his position and round the back of the car. Shots rang out and then there was silence.

I got to my feet and charged over, rounding the front of the vehicle while Franky, I could see, went around the back. We found Micky standing over the two other guys who had been shot up and dead.

"Bloody hell, Micky, that was a bold move," I said.

"Figured I muffed my first shot and didn't take out the driver so had a bit of making up to do," he replied, looking over the two dead soldiers.

I made my way to the jeep and looked in where both the lads nearest too us had copped for the original attack and probably shielded the other two guys who had been able to

106

fight back. The car itself didn't look in too good a nick as smoke was billowing from the bonnet.

"Jesus wept, Micky, what did you do lob a couple of grenades in the jeep? I hope the bloody thing still works as we are knackered if it doesn't," I said.

We inspected the car and started to take everything out. Micky tried the ignition but nothing from the engine; it looked like it was damaged beyond repair.

"Shit," I said, banging my fists against the bonnet. "We are in no better position than we were before."

"Yeah, but look at this one, he looks like a bit of a senior bloke though, dressed up in his fancy uniform, so not a complete failure," said Franky.

"What the heck was he doing out here then?" I said. "Let's get everything out of the car and see what we can use; hopefully, there's some grub and water."

Chapter 20

There was. A canteen of water had survived and some cans of food. The biggest bonus though was a couple of spare fuel cans, the only problem is we had two vehicles none of which were operational. We looked through the rest of the things. Franky was trying to force open the top of a can about a two-foot-long and a foot high. Looked like an old ammunition tin I was thinking but it was very heavy, so there was something in it. The top came off and Franky let out a whistle, which wasn't the easiest of thing to do out here in this dry desert with dry lips.

"Jesus, lads you are not going to believe what I have found. It's like Christmas day in the bank of Ireland." He delved his hands in the box and brought out two handfuls of gold!!! It shimmered in the late desert sun and was almost blinding as we all stood there looking at it.

Me and Micky wandered over and peered in. There was hundreds of coins in this dusty old box and I picked one up looking at it closely. "Not only does it appear to look like gold, lads, but it looks really old. Like something out of history or something," I said.

"Too bloody right it is," said Franky. "We are rich, boys, rich I tell you."

"Yeah rich boys," I said. "Stranded out here in the middle of nowhere. Fine bloody good that's going to do us. We can't exactly use it to buy us a car now, can we?"

"We'll figure it out," said Franky.

"OK, let's get back to our camp. This car is in worse shape than ours. We'll take the rations, water and petrol back with us and think on our next move overnight."

"And my gold," said Franky closing the top down on the bottom and making sure it was all in there.

"Aye and our gold," I said with a big grin on my face.

We got back to the jeep with the newly acquired stores and had a brew while we all examined the coins. On one side, they had like a crouching warrior, something like that, with what I thought looked like a bow and arrow. On the other side, it was hard to make out it could have been a head. They were beautiful and were gold and looked extremely old.

"So, the million-pound question is how do we get out of here, get back to base in one piece, report back to the boss and carry out this box of treasure, ensuring we enjoy our retirement after the war?" I said.

"Well, we have provisions and we can take turns carrying the box, its only 80 to 100 miles," said Franky optimistically. One thing for sure was he wasn't leaving the gold behind.

"And even if we miraculously survive all that, do you think they will let us keep all this booty for ourselves," I said.

"What I don't understand is what were those Jerrys doing with it in the car out here in the first place," said Micky.

"Nazi's Micky, they are famous for robbing every precious artefact they can lay their hands on. I have heard they all get shipped back to Hitler and he has warehouses full of priceless antiques, as much wealth as the world has ever seen," said Franky.

"Yeah, I heard the same," I said.

"Well we have two fuel cans and I reckon I could have a go at trying to fix the tank on our jeep," said Micky. "If I can fix it, we can make a dash for it back to base and worry about the gold later."

"Do you reckon you can?" I said.

"Yeah, if it's a bullet whole we have plenty of stuff we can use to patch it up. These are four-gallon tins so we should have enough fuel to get back," he said. "And we could also drain the tank off the Jerry car over there for a bit extra."

"All right, let's get some sleep then and try the fix in the morning," I said.

With that, we all bedded down to try and get some sleep. I was pondering the problem of getting the gold back in a way that we could keep it to ourselves for a little nest egg after the war. I fell asleep thinking of what I would spend it on.

Chapter 21

We woke fresh and early and managed to jack the jeep up on a temporary ramp of rocks and stones. Micky slid under it and we left him to it.

"You know, Franky, I have been pondering what we can do with that gold. If we stroll back into camp with it, it'll disappear, and some big knob will end up with it."

"I know we are not letting that happen, Vic."

"I agree and the only solution I can think of is that we don't walk back into camp with it."

"What you are saying, leave it out here? No bloody way, mate, it's ours, finders' keepers and all that."

"No, I agree, mate. What I was thinking is we stash it somewhere and come back for it later. You know when either we go back to blighty from here or even, if we have too, after the war."

"OK, I buy that but where the hell could we stash it out here in the desert. Somewhere where you could find it again?"

"That, my old mate, is exactly the right question," I said as I raised my hands in the air. We sat there for a long time thinking through the problem.

Franky jumped up. "I think I have an idea. Do you remember that garrison we passed at the foot of that mountain on our way out here? Mount, oh what was it called?"

"Mount Himeimat," I said.

"That's it. So, we make our way back to that camp and bed down there while we get running repairs done on the jeep before we go onto our base. While we are there, we can go up on the mountain and I bet there are loads of places to stash the gold. Sound like a plan?"

"Sounds feasible and probably the best one we have. All we need now is for Micky to fix the bloody jeep."

He spent most of the morning working on it while I got some relief in the shade out of the sun having a kip. Franky spent the time playing with the gold. Micky wandered over. "Right, I think I have cracked it, we just need to get it off the ramps and then try it out with the fuel," he said.

We jumped up to help and rolled the jeep into place. While we did this, we talked through our plan for the gold. Micky was OK with it if we thought it was our only plan. Micky watched the tank carefully while I poured in the fuel. There was a couple of bubbles on the outside of the tank, but it seemed to be holding.

"All right!" shouted Micky. "I will go and get the other fuel out of the Jerry car and be back in a bit if you blokes load up."

We loaded the jeep keeping the gold in the front with us. Micky returned and we strapped the additional fuel to the jeep and set off back towards Mount Himeimat. It was slow progress and every now and again, we would stop to check the fuel gauge and tank. There was a bit of leakage from the tank, but it was holding. We went as far as we dared that night before making camp. We did see an aircraft off in the distance which reminded us of our original mission that had completely slipped our mind and we decided to start recording activity again. We also decided to mention the shootout with the Germans and the senior ranked bloke but of course we were not mentioning anything of any gold.

The next morning, we used the fuel from the second spare drum and set off. We expected to get there by dusk, but the going was slow, and we were still short and forced to make camp again for a second night of the return leg. We poured the last of the fuel in the following morning and set off making our destination just after lunchtime. We reported to the garrison commander and he issued us with tent space while the mechanics set about repairing the various issues with our jeep. The damn thing had been brilliant and literally saved our life. We took ALL our belongings with us into the tent, including the dusty old box and bunked down for the afternoon to catch up on some much-needed sleep.

Franky woke me in the early evening, "Vic, it's time we went up on the mountain and stashed the box, mate."

It was surprisingly easy for three blokes to walk out of camp with a box and up into the slopes of the mountain. We expected to be challenged and had prepared stories of what we were up to, but no one seemed to care. I guess with war raging and blokes all over the place, we just didn't look like we were up to anything unusual. The chaos of war I guess worked in our favour! We stashed the box and returned to camp without incident. Surprisingly easy was the feeling when we crashed onto the beds.

"Right, should we write down where we have stashed it, a treasure map if you like," I said.

"No chance," said Franky. "It could easily get into the wrong hands. I have the exact directions up here," he said pointing to his head. "When the time is right, I will write it down for us, but this just isn't the right place." He was right. There were several blokes within ear shot in the tent.

"All right, I'm happy with that," I said. Franky was the one guy I trusted more than anyone in the world.

Chapter 22

The second Battle of El Alamein as it was now known had been a huge success for the Allies. We had driven Rommel right out of Egypt, and he was continuing his retreat across Libya. Looking back now, I am hugely proud of the fact that we played our part in it. We arrived in Africa and had no time to think about it before we were thrust into the teeth of the fight. Not once but twice and had lived to tell the tail.

After leaving the Mount Himeimat area, we hooked back up with the captain who wasn't totally impressed with out sighting notes. I think he was a bit sceptical about the dust up with the Germans as well but nevertheless he seemed glad we had returned. Looking at German uniform pictures, it looked like we had taken out an Oberstleutnant (Lieutenant Colonel) so we were well pleased with ourselves. There didn't seem to be any medals on offer though!

We had given up on the prospect of joining the Irish Brigade as we had found out from the captain that they hadn't come to Egypt at all, and in fact were part of a different operation in Algiers. They had landed there with the Americans, who I didn't even know were in this war, as part of a cunning plan to attack the enemy from the west as well as the east. That sounded good to me and I wouldn't have wanted to be Rommel trapped in both directions! The captain had swung it that we could stay with the New Zealand unit which was fine by us. The New Zealand lads had always made us feel very welcome and we felt part of their family after all we had been through together.

We found ourselves in a period of quiet, the quiet before the storm was the un-nerving feeling. It was time to recuperate in both mind and spirit and I certainly took my time to catch up on some much-needed sleep. It was also a time where it seemed we were building up our forces and more and more equipment and ammunition arrived every day. The rumour was we were resuming the push west in December to finally kick the Germans and Italians out of Africa for good. Well, if that was the case, we were up for it.

It was incredible to think we had only been in Africa for six weeks or so but felt like veterans of the campaign. Dublin seemed a million miles away and having waited two years to get involved, we certainly could now say we knew what war was all about. I still hadn't got used to the heat, although loads of the lads strolled around topless in the sun, working on their tans, it wasn't for me. I tried it a few times and found I still burned so most of my down time was spent hunkering down in the shade or on my bunk in the tent I shared obviously with Micky and Franky but also three other blokes.

It was a special time that, just relaxing in the desert with your mates, larking around and basically being your own man. Never through the rest of my life had I felt so content as I did in those couple of weeks the three of us spent together. It would seem strange to anyone who hadn't been through what we had been through and come out the other side, that in the middle of a war, you just felt so alive and happy with life. I suppose it was having no other concerns than staying alive. There was no worry of finding work, paying the bills, pressure on what you were going to do with your life and trying to find love! All that just didn't matter in the desert.

We spoke regularly about the gold coins and how we would try and get them out of Africa but plan as we might, we just couldn't think of a way to do it. While we were with the rest of the platoon under the eyes of the captain and the sarge, there was just no way. Our only plan then was to hope it remained safe and hidden and to come back after the war and collect it. That's presuming there would be an 'after the war' as no one knew at that time whether it would end. It might just go on for decades. We thought though we could get Jerry out of Africa and even if they occupied Europe, it still may mean freedom of travel to Africa and the chance to come back for the gold. Franky still hadn't written down the details for recovery, but we were relaxed about it.

One afternoon, while we were relaxing on our bunks the mail arrived. "Letter for you, Mulligan," came the shout and a letter was tossed over to me. I started to open it, must be news from Dublin from Ma. I had written a week back so was probably due a reply. But it wasn't.

"Hey, boys, it's from Huck; would you believe?" I said.

"Yeah, great news, mate, great that he made it. What's he got to say for himself then," said Franky and both him and Micky sat up to listen as I read aloud the letter.

Hey there Vic,

I wanted to drop you a note to say thanks for getting me off that battlefield and to let you know I was alive!

I can't remember what happened that day. I just remember us working our way forward and firing like mad at the enemy. I remember thinking we are doing alright here boys and then the next thing I was on a plane out of Africa. I hear in the papers the battle went well and we are winning so at least it wasn't in vein.

Although I am alive Vic I haven't fared too well. I lost my right leg just below the knee and I have no feeling in my right arm. I am writing this with my left arm so don't take the piss out of the state of my writing. They tell me I have a few more month's recuperation here in the hospital and then I will be allowed to make the journey back home. I have received letters from my family, they are really upset but glad I am alive.

Anyhow I hope you blokes are all OK. I heard you literally carried me miles back out of there. I will always be in your debt. Please pass on my regards to Micky and Franky.

Regards

Finn (Huckleberry)

"Ahh good on him sounds like he has a really rough time," said Franky.

"What's he mean you carried him out of the battle? As I remember it, I did all the bloody hard work. You couldn't carry my mam across the street, Vic," said Micky.

"Yeah, credit where it's due, Micky, you played a bloody blinder that night, mate," I said.

"You know," said Franky, "if we get out of this alive and get the gold back to blighty somehow, then we should send him some money. He's one of our gang, and he's bloody earnt it."

"Yeah agree with that, mate, sounds like he will need it as well. Probably be in a bloody wheelchair for the rest of his life," said Micky. "Can you imagine that? He was only here a few weeks and now has to go back to the other side of the world in a wheelchair."

"I know and he mentions his family in the letter. Bet it's difficult for them to get their head around a war that's thousands of miles away and could never affect them directly. It's like all the other lads here we have spent time with, hats off to them I say," said Franky.

"Great shout, boys, that's definitely a deal then," I said. I folded the letter and put it in my top pocket. I read it a few times through the rest of the war, especially in the down times. I found it so inspiring that a young bloke who had been through hell took the time to write such a nice letter, in the middle of all this madness, to thank me. I felt very humble and very proud. It also struck me that he would be as far away in the world as you could be down there in New Zealand, and that we were not likely to see each other again.

Chapter 23

The quiet period lasted about three weeks. The sarge popped into the tent one evening and said to get ready for a briefing in an hour's time. We all gathered around the captain and the map of the region.

"Right, if you didn't think you have had enough excitement so far in this war, then you are definitely going to get it over the next week or so. Jerry is now well and truly out of Egypt and we have the whole 8th Army sat on the border waiting to send him scarpering. You could not but have noticed the huge build-up of troops and vehicles over the last few weeks and now it's time to use it. Most of the action is up here along the northern coast road," he said, using his stick to point to the map.

"Now we know Rommel hasn't had time to prepare defensive lines across Libya so simply won't be able to stand up to the assault we have planned for him. Most of the 8th Army will attack across the north at first light and will hope to get Jerry on the run. Actually, I say Jerry but most of the rumours are that they have pulled out and in fact, it will be mostly the Italians carrying out a fighting retreat. Don't get too complacent with that though, they have really been showing some metal in North Africa now the Germans have shown them how to fight. Now while all this is going on along the coast, we are going to make a fast-mechanised dash for El Aghella over here further around the coast. The idea is we cut off the retreating Rommel and trap him from both sides where we can finish them off once and for all." He looked around at us all although no one gave anything away about how we were feeling about this.

He carried on, "I know it's ambitious and a bit daunting. After all, if we make it in time, we are likely to be getting the whole of Rommel's fleeing army right in the face and they are going to fight like wounded animals to get past us. I have seen how tenacious we are in the heat of battle and have every confidence of doing the job asked of us. Any questions?"

One of the lads at the back of the party asked, "How far is it, Captain, that looks like a heck of a trip."

"It's about three hundred and eighty miles and the terrain isn't great. We expect it to take us about three days to get there and we will have to be ready for the fight as soon as we get near the coast. If we make it before Rommel, we may well have time to dig in and be prepared, but let's not bank on that. We might have to simply attack their flank on the move.

Either way, it's not going to be easy but if it goes our way, could just deliver that decisive victory we are looking for. Any more questions, gentlemen?"

Everyone shook their heads. I was thinking, wow this really is driving into the teeth of the storm. If I had been looking for action in Dublin, then this was certainly going to be it.

"OK, we need to spend the night loading up the trucks with as much supplies as we can. Each truck will need to carry its own fuel, platoon of men and their rations and ammunition. Once we set out, the supply chain will be stretched and unable to keep up for a number of days so we will be on our own. Let's move, gentlemen, there is a lot to do," he shouted to add a bit of emphasis. "We set off at first light."

We all trundled out and back to the tents to get our kit together. I crammed as much food and water as I could get into my kit. My thinking being if we were in the trucks, we wouldn't have far to carry it anyhow. Micky had acquired a heavy machine gun and had been practicing during the down time and he now started to load that in our truck with boxes of ammunition. There wasn't much room for us blokes but none of us wanted to get caught out in the desert short of food and water and from what the captain was saying, we would be needing a fair bit of ammunition. We got back to our bunks in the early hours for a few hours kip before setting out.

In the dark, Franky spoke, "This is a daring campaign and no mistake, fellas."

"I don't mind the action when we get there and get stuck into them. It's the three days in the back of that truck my arse isn't looking forward too," I said. They all chuckled at that and incredibly, with such excitement to come, we all fell asleep for a few hours.

We were up at first light. No need for alarm clocks with all the racket going on. Our platoon mounted up with me, Franky and Micky occupying the tailgate positions as had become a custom on these missions. We pulled out eating breakfast rations on the way. It was a fantastic sight, vehicles as far as the eye could see all moving in convoy. If all was to go to plan, we wouldn't see the enemy until day three and that's how it turned out from our vantage point in the truck. You could hear a terrific battle going off somewhere and I guessed that must be the assault in the North. Let's hope they were occupying them and giving us time to get there before they did.

I was right about my backside; that was the most un-comfiest rides of my life and we were all a bit fed up and banged around by the time we approached our target. There was a pause in the drive while we readied ourselves for battle. The sarge briefed us to be on our metal, as we would reach the coast road in the next few hours and this was where it was going to get tasty. We were on hyper alert for them last few miles I can tell you. We started to hear the sounds of battle as the first elements of our attack engaged the enemy. I remember thinking they must have got the shock of their lives to see this armada of trucks pouring out of the desert towards them. They thought the biggest threat was behind them!

We tangled with their forward formations and broke into their lines. They halted their advance and we managed to bog them down. "Dig In, dig in," shouted the sarge as we started to make our stand. The enemy stood off probably amazed to see us and try and work out what they were going to do next. This brief stalemate gave us chance to dig in before they threw themselves at us. We were well prepared and let them have everything. It was one hell of a fight before they withdrew. To us the trap had worked, and we had them.

Chapter 24

Skirmishes went on all day before the sarge called us out of the line and back into the truck. "What the hell's going on, Sarge?" I said.

"Rommel has twigged onto to our road-block here. We are getting reports they have broken up into smaller units and are bypassing us inland cross country. They are using the firm terrain we used to get here. We must get some units back in-land and engage them there. We have been chosen as one of those units so let's get moving. Everyone be on their metal as the plan is fluid from here. We will engage them as find them," he said, directing everyone back into the truck.

We set off again in the middle of the battle but not in the orderly formations we had held over the last three days. Separate trucks and armour were setting out as soon as they had loaded up. Still there were enough to look impressive. We were literally an army on the move.

We were going about an hour when the world simply turned upside down. There was an almighty explosion and I was flung from the back of the truck as the whole thing seemed to jump in the air like a dolphin and plunge to the sand on its side. As I hit the ground, my right shoulder took the full force of my body and just gave away. I landed in a heap and cried out in pain. It was absolutely excruciating. My kit and bags falling all around me and I was winded from the contact with the ground. I lay dazed on the ground for some time until I started to get my senses together and take in the scene around me.

When I did, I found the whole of my right arm was just dangling loose. I couldn't work out if I had been shot but I couldn't find any blood anywhere. I can't describe the shooting pains in my shoulder. I rolled onto my front to try and work out what was going on. To my right was the overturned truck with five or six blokes crouched behind it firing like mad. I looked to my left and saw an enemy emplacement. They had dug in and there were several of them and they had a heavy machine gun. They were strafing the truck and bullets were flying everywhere.

I turned back to the truck where the guys were. I could see Micky; he looked OK and was firing back with his heavy machine gun. Without the truck shielding them, they would have been massacred. It was then I realised I was out in the open. If they turned their guns on me, I had had it. I looked further round and saw Franky. He was rolling around screaming in pain. He must have taken a round and he was as exposed as I was. I almost wanted to tell him to shut up and not attract any attention our way.

I tried crawling but the pain in my shoulder stopped me in my tracks. This was a pretty desperate position to be in. All I could do is keep my head down and hope the lads won the fight. I looked towards Micky and he stared at me. He understood straight away the predicament me and Franky were in. I will never forget that frightened look in his eyes. Micky was never frightened. He took a couple of grenades out and seem to wait. What was he doing?

The heavy machine gun stopped probably during reloading, and he jumped up. The rest of the lads continued firing as he raced round the truck and dived towards the enemy lobbing both grenades in their den. They didn't see them coming and there was a couple of explosions followed by screams and all sorts of debris flew out of the whole. I watched as the rest of the lads rounded the truck and fired with everything they had into the enemy as they reached their emplacement and jumped in the firing stopped.

The silence was eerie. I dragged myself to a sitting position, hanging onto my shoulder and then onto my knees crawling across to Franky. He was swearing for all he was worth which I took as a good sign. "What's up with you, you big girl?" I said.

"Been shot in my bloody arm, haven't I! Jesus, it hurts. It's bleeding like a flooded damn," he said as he noticed my shoulder. "What's up with you?"

"Don't know, think I must have dislocated the shoulder, it's bloody agony. My whole arm's dead."

We helped each other to our feet and shuffled across to the truck. There were several of the guys lying dead in there. Whatever had hit us, they had borne the brunt of it and had no chance. The good thing I thought was that at least they didn't see it coming.

A couple of the guys came around the truck. "We shut those bastards up anyway. Anyone else alive in here?" said one of the guys called Brendan.

"Doesn't look like it," I said.

"All right, I will check it out. You two don't look so clever either. Get yourselves over into their dugout. We will have to make a stand for it in there until help arrives," said Brendan.

"Micky made the breakthrough with those grenades, what a brave move that was," I said

"Yeah, he was one of the bravest lads I ever knew. Should be pinning medals on him for that."

"I will go and see if he's OK," I said.

"Oh, sorry Vic," he said. He looked absolutely gutted. "He took a number of shots making his break for it. He's dead, mate! He is over there near the dugout. I'm sorry mate I know you guys were close, " As he walked passed me he patted me on my shoulder.

Me and Franky just stood there; we couldn't believe what we had heard. Somehow, we almost felt indestructible, the three of us. We marched off over to where Micky lay. He had taken four bullets to the chest and hadn't stood a chance. "What a bloody hero he was, Franky. He could see we were right out in the open, that's why he did it, the bloody fool." I struggled to hold it together I had just never felt anything like it.

Franky was too choked up to reply.

Brendan came back. "Sorry about Micky, lads," he said, pausing, feeling a bit of a spare part in this little scene. After a few seconds, he said, "The sarge and everyone else in the truck are dead. With you two, there are seven survivors. Let's get into that hole and set up a defensive position."

We reluctantly had to leave Micky and jump into the cover of the hole. The lads had turned the enemy machine gun round pointing out into the direction we expected them to come from. The same had been done with Micky's heavy machine gun. We looked around the dugout and collected all the guns and ammo we could. We also made a couple of journeys to the truck to load up with more of the stores from there. There was a kind of grenade launcher in the dugout which I guessed must have been the sucker that took out our truck.

Chapter 25

When we had the defences in order, the guys assessed the pair of us. We had medical supplies and they patched Franky's arm up and stopped the bleeding and put it in a sling. He had stopped moaning though as I guess we both realised whatever our injuries, it was nothing compared to poor Micky. I know for me, I also realised if Micky hadn't done what he did, I might not have survived at all and that was a very sobering thought.

"Vic, you have definitely dislocated that shoulder," said Kane, one of the other blokes. "I am going to have to shove it back in place. Do you want some morphine to ease the pain?"

"No chance, don't give me any of that. I need my wits about me in case we get ambushed here. Have you got any booze?" I said.

"Got some brandy, take a few mouthfuls of that and get yourself ready," he said.

Which I most certainly did. He grabbed my arm and I braced myself as the other blokes held me down. "OK, after three," he said. "One Two." And then, he whacked it back into place. I jumped a mile and shouted every curse I could think of.

When I finally got my breath back, I said, "What the hell happened to three?"

"Always better to surprise a bloke when doing something like that. The tendons will have taken a hammering, so it's going to be painful and you won't be able to use it for a while. I will strap it up to give it some support, but you got months of rehabilitation with that, mate, I'm afraid."

"Great," I said and lay back to get my breath back for a few minutes, taking a few more gulps of brandy. Every time I have smelled a brandy since then, it always reminds me of that moment and I involuntarily always grab my shoulder.

It was getting dark now, so we arranged ourselves into two shifts of guard duty, splitting up myself and Franky as we only had the use of one arm. The truck was still smouldering behind us and I guess that steered the enemy trucks away from us. We could hear them passing at various points in the night, but we never got any eyes on them to engage them with fire.

It was a long night looking out there in the dark, waiting for the enemy to come flying in. While I was awake, I vigorously peered out there. It helped me clear my mind and not think of Micky. I grabbed a few hours' sleep, waking a couple of times as a few of the blokes opened up at enemy vehicles passing by but they were too far away to hit.

As the sun came up, we reassessed the situation. You could see smoke in various places across the desert. We had enough stores and weapons to last a few days but with the truck burning, we had no way of driving back to safety.

Our plan was simple. If the 8th Army were all over the back of the enemy and chasing them across the desert, then it couldn't be too long before the battle reached us. As we saw it, we would then have two options. First, the enemy would attack us in which case, we would fight for our lives but probably wouldn't get out alive. Or second, they would simply bypass our position and we would be rescued by our guys chasing on their heels. Obviously, the hope was for option two but too be honest, I wasn't that bothered. I really wanted to shoot anything I could. These lot had killed Micky and life wouldn't ever be the same again.

It was mid-morning when I was sat with Franky. "This is too quiet," I said. "The enemy has to be out there somewhere; they couldn't have all got back through our lines."

"I know. I have this feeling bloody loads of them are going to come barrelling out of the dust and just run right over us."

"Do you want something to eat?"

"Yeah, what do we have, have we got any steak and chips?"

"Afraid not, mate, its canned meat and stale biscuits again but at least we have a brew on." I pulled out the rations and gave them to Franky and we started to open them.

"It's really weird not having Micky here, Vic. Bloody gutted, mate, it's been a heck of a year with him."

"Yeah, breaks your heart, Franky. That's why we got to get out of here and make his heroics all worthwhile. There are seven blokes here who might not be alive if he hadn't taken out those Jerrys."

"Do you remember that night back in Dublin when we all ended up spending a night in the clink? Seems a lifetime ago now, doesn't it?"

"Yeah, a different world, wasn't it?" I said. "Mind you, it was the start of a beautiful friendship."

"Got vehicles coming in pretty fast from the north," shouted Brendan.

"Here we go, Franky, let's give them some pain," I said, climbing to my feet.

We had practiced that morning and had worked out me and Franky could work Micky's heavy machine gun and get it loaded so it was decided we would take that and the other guys would be better using all the other weaponry we had at our disposal. We took up our positions and waited looking, out at the dust clouds making their way towards us.

"All right, chaps," said Kane. "Hold your fire until they get in close enough and then let them have everything you have got."

The tension was unbearable, but I was just keen to fire as many bullets as I could. Brendan had picked up the Grenade launcher and was going to have a go with that. We waited on his mark for the kick-off. They were a couple of hundred yards out when BANG, the grenade launcher blasted out and we all opened up. We couldn't really see exactly what we were shooting at, but they were in formation and veered right when they saw our firepower on them. The grenade burst well short but had created an impact of panic on a fleeing enemy who had been looking behind them up until that point.

It was clear they didn't fancy taking us on. Their priority was to move as fast as they could back towards their own lines and safety. They passed at a hundred yards or so to the east and fired back as they did. They had some heavy firepower as well but fortunately for us, it wasn't too accurate. There must have been at least twenty vehicles in the convoy, and they passed us very quickly. As they passed to the south of us, they disappeared behind our burnt-out truck and we ceased firing. A few of us scrambled out of the dugout and ran over the truck to see the dust clouds disappearing off to the south.

The whole engagement couldn't have lasted more than five or six minutes. I have absolutely no idea if we managed to inflict any casualties on them, but we certainly gave them a fright.

We had two more similar engagements during the rest of the day, but nothing got too close to be too much of a concern to us and our safety. We seemed far more relaxed as the evening drew in as I guess we knew what to expect having already been through a night out here. I reckon I probably got four or five hours sleep which seemed to confirm our mood of optimism.

It was the following afternoon when we finally hooked up with the rest of the British troops. Fortunately, we had not shot them up when they came out of the desert as they were clearly flying Union Jacks, so we climbed out of our hide hole and waved them in. What a great site that was and we met them like long lost family relatives.

I was well proud of our little bunch. There didn't seem to have been any nerves amongst us, we were all ready to fight to the end. Although our objectives were supposed to stop their escape and of course we hadn't managed to do that, but I reckoned we had given a good account of ourselves and couldn't have done anymore.

That's when the sadness of Micky's demise hit us again and we agreed with the lads to get the rest of our team who had been killed and bury them out there in the desert. That was a very solemn occasion as the seven survivors stood round the graves of our lost colleagues. We stood there for ages before finally turning away and heading for our ride out of there leaving behind our buddy.

Chapter 26

We ended up back at base camp only a lot further into Libya than we had been before. It was clear the enemy were definitely on the run and our experiences of them scarpering past us in the desert would back that up. We heard the offensive had finally come to a halt short of Tripoli by Christmas Day, but it certainly looked like a stunning victory. The 8th Army had covered hundreds of miles in only a few weeks. Considering how long we had been fighting in Egypt, it was remarkable that we skipped across Libya in such a short time.

I bet the big boys were clapping themselves on the back and handing out medals to each other for their bold planning. From our point of view, we knew how hard we had fought on the ground and we had seen many colleagues not come out of that desert, so there was certainly no celebrating and partying on our account.

When we arrived back in camp, it was obvious that mine and Franky's war in Africa had come to an end. Both of us, with our right arms bandaged and in slings, looked a right sight. We spent a week in the medical unit at camp which was full of soldiers in far worse states than ourselves. To be honest, I felt a bit of a fraud as I only really had a painful shoulder and I was on enough drugs and alcohol to ensure it didn't really bother me too much. As it turned out, Kane's diagnosis back there during the battle was accurate. I had completely shot all the tendons and muscles in my shoulder and was going to need a lot of rest and recuperation, followed by physio, to get it back to working order.

The doctor told me my war wasn't over, but it certainly was for the foreseeable future and that was all right by me. I was fed up of the desert by now and there is nowhere like home at Christmas time. Cold, dark and wet nights. Lovely and couldn't be more different than this place.

Franky's diagnosis was a little more serious, but he would recover in time and, therefore, available to re-join the war if he wanted too. He had had a serious bullet pass straight through his upper arm but the doctors out there in the desert had managed to save the arm to which we were all thankful. He was now stitched up and once healed he would gain almost 100% of the use of the arm. Overall, we had been very lucky. We had taken part in three battles and the skirmish with the Jerry car while on patrol since arriving in Africa, and it looked like we had come through it. Obviously the same couldn't be said about Micky and we were extremely glum about that.

We were told we were to fly out back to Britain on a transport plane carrying the wounded the following morning. Once we landed in Britain, we would be assessed and given further orders from there.

"So that really is it, Franky, we are going home, mate," I said.

"Yeah and not before time, Vic, I am knackered now!" he replied.

"How long have we been here?"

"Well, it must be just over three months now I guess, something like that. Can you believe it? It feels like a lifetime doesn't it?"

"Yeah, we have certainly seen some things in the last two months. We have definitely grown up now, mate."

"You know if Micky was here with us and getting on that plane, we would be partying right now. What a bloody waste that is but typical of the bloke he went out in a blaze of glory," said Franky.

"You are not wrong there, old mate, we owe him our lives and I, for one, intend to make the most of it."

"Yeah talking of the future, I wonder what it has install for us when we get back?"

"Been thinking about that, mate. I want to go back to Dublin to see the folks while my arm is on the mend, but I want to get back into this war as soon as I can. There is no way I am going to sit in Dublin while this lot is going on after what Micky sacrificed for his family," I said. "But I don't want to drag you back into it, mate, if it's not for you. You had a really lucky escape there and I don't blame you if you think you have done your bit."

"Bollocks to that thought, Vic. There's a Jerry or an Italian out there that nearly took my arm off. There's no way I am sitting out the rest of the fight. Where and when you go, Vic, I will be there with you, mate."

I couldn't help smiling at the bloke for that. It's difficult to explain to people how powerful a friendship like that can be and I patted him on his good arm with my good arm! I was so proud of him and had so much love for the bloke at that moment. "I knew you would say that, mate, but I was rather hoping to shake you off you are becoming very clingy and a pain in the butt," I said, laughing.

Franky was laughing back now, "Sorry, mate, you don't get rid of me that easy."

"The other thing we haven't discussed is the gold. It seems a million miles away now and I guess we will have to give it up if we are leaving Africa for good. Egypt is miles away, mate."

"Yeah, I thought of that, Vic, as well. The only option left to us is if we survive this war, and we don't know how long it's going to rumble on for, we come back for it. Both of us like together and split it down the middle. If one of us doesn't make it, then the other gets the lot. If we both cop it, then it will stay there until some lucky bugger stumbles over it, one day."

"Can't argue with that logic although if I get the chance, I would like to bung Micky's mum some of the loot. I think she deserves it; after all, it was the death of his brother that finally got us off our backside and into the war."

"Yeah, didn't think of that. Just think she has lost both boys now. She must be devastated. Vic, it's typical of you to think of that. And don't forget we said we would also send some down to Huck after his misfortunes." Franky offered me his hand to shake and I shook it. "OK, it's a deal then."

"The only issue is remembering where we hid it," I said.

"That's easy enough I remember it all up here," he said pointing to his head. "But I think the time has come to write it all down for a treasure hunt in the future."

"OK," I said. "I can still write with this bloody arm. You shout out the details and I will jot down two copies, one for you and one for me. That way we both have the details and if we cop it, then the directions cop it with us."

"OK, here we go," said Franky.

We approached the mount from our base in the southwest following a 45 degree path (not sure that's relevant but captured it anyway)

When we reached the mount, we tracked the base of it east until we saw the little mount.

Mount Himeimat is easily identified from its unique geological features. It consists of two mounts, a big and smaller one.

Continue into the valley between the two mounts with the larger mount on your left-hand side.

In the centre of the valley, there will be a rough path that makes the climb to the top easier. (there are a couple of other paths just inside the valley – ignore them and take the 3rd path) We didn't measure how far into the valley we walked but it looked halfway to both ends.

Use the path to climb to the top of Mount Himeimat. It's quite steep in places and we found this difficult in the dark.

Once on top, measure 120 paces in a west direction. That will give you the depth into the mount before turning north and walking to the rim of the mountaintop.

From there, scramble down the side 14 feet to a ledge and then turn to your left.

There are many small caves and ridges that run along here. I counted 23 paces on my way back from where we buried the treasure.

There is a prominent rock next to it and you scratched a V on it, Vic as a guide. The treasure was buried here in the small ridge in the face of the mountain.

V & F, December 1942

And with that, we were ready to leave. Flying out of Africa was such a relief but it wasn't then end of our war or our adventures, but those stories will have to wait for another time.

Part 3
October 1991 Manchester

Chapter 27

Glenn waited a few days for Brian to come back to him. In fact, he waited four. What was he doing? Surely, he could have read it by now. Brian rang on the evening of the fourth day.

"Cracking story that, mate," he said. "I can't believe Granddad wrote that but typical of the life I always pictured him having that's for sure. It's brilliant!"

"So, what do you think?" asked Glenn, "Do we follow it up?"

"Too right we do, what the hell, he has left enough money to do it. Can't very well go and spend it on a new car when he saved it up for this cause. Those guys went through hell and back to win that gold and we owe them at least a try to see if it's still there. Plus, I haven't ever been further than the Costa del Sol! So yeah count me in," was his very enthusiastic reply.

"All right, cool, let me look into arrangements, flights hotel, etc. and I will come back to you and we can plan it from there."

"Sounds good. I thought I knew loads about the war but some of the stories he tells were new to me, Glenn. I fancy following them up further at some point. Like the bombing of Dublin, who knew about that? I thought they were always neutral in the war, then you find out the Germans bombed it."

"That is unbelievable, my thoughts exactly. In fact, while I have been waiting for you to read the story at your snail's pace, I went down to the library in Manchester on my lunch break and read some old newspapers stories about it. It's absolutely full on true and just how Granddad described it. I can't believe he was there right in the middle of it."

"Right, neither can I. In a way, I am glad he was though as it shaped the rest of his life. As he said, he never went back to live in Dublin after he left."

"The other thing I found out from the articles that I couldn't believe is that it looks like it was bombed in error. A Germen pilot got off target and thought it was Belfast! Dropped his bombs on the wrong city."

"Jesus, that is unbelievable. So, if Victor was accurate with that bit of the story, then we have got to accept Glenn that the whole story he told was true," said Brian.

"It is, mate. Well, I think it is. I bought a book from WH Smiths called the 'Chronicles of the Second World War'. It's a cracking read and details what happened in the war day by day. Obviously, I haven't had chance to read it in detail, but I focussed in on some of the dates Granddad mentioned and there were battles going on in the places; he seems to indicate."

"There you go then; it's got to be true. You know what I regret though, I wish we had taken the time to sit down with him and talk through it all. It's a great story in detail but we could have asked him loads of questions as we went through it."

"I know. I feel like we never even knew him. I would have loved to have known him when he was our age, which seems to be the case in the stories he wrote. Did he ever mention Franky or Micky to you or even indicate that he had been in Egypt?"

"Never mentioned a word, mate. Look what he and his mates did at not much of an older age than we are now. So we shouldn't be daunted by going over there in the 1990s; it's not as if there will be people shooting at us, is it?"

"OK, it's agreed then. We go."

"Right, I need to get off this phone. You know Dad, he charges us for all the calls so I am running up a bill here I can't afford to pay," said Brian.

"We need a planning meeting. Why don't you come around Friday night, we can have a few beers and plan out the whole trip? I will get a map of North Egypt which should help.

They sell them in WH Smiths as well. Should have got one the other day."

"All right, Glenn, see you Friday night," said Brian and hung up.

So, the trips on, thought Glenn. *Lots to do now to get ready for Friday night's session.* He made a mental note to make sure they got all the decisions made before they drank too many beers. He had banked the cheque from the solicitor for the four grand Granddad had left him. That would be the money to use for all the expenses.

He went and got a pad and paper and started two lists. On one, he started jotting down the things he needed to do and get decisions on with Brian. On the other, he started to record all the expenses so they could hopefully do everything within the four grand. Neither him nor Brian had any spare cash to spend on the adventure so he would work to the budget Victor had set.

The following day's lunch hour would be busy so he had let his supervisor know he would probably take a couple of hours flexi time and come back late. The first task on his list was to pick up a map of Egypt and pop into the travel agent's. He was going to try and get hold of a brochure on holidays in Egypt and ask a few questions if need be. It will help with looking at the costs and it would also help them make some decisions.

The first thing was the map and he found what he was looking for reasonably quickly. Well, it wasn't a map of Egypt, it was the whole of Africa, but you could see enough detail of Egypt when it was all folded out. £1.89 so it would be the first cost on the list. Not too much of a dent into the four grand, so he was happy enough with that. He could hear Brian moaning that they would be watching the pounds when they had thousands to spend. Glenn was much more conservative with money and, therefore, he knew it would be down to him to keep track on it or it would run away from them.

The travel agent's was much more interesting. He figured they would need to be there for a week so was looking for package holidays. However, these all seemed geared up around visiting the pyramids and he realised they were probably the only people going to that part of the world that weren't interested in looking at pyramids!

So, the travel agent advised it would be better booking flights separately and then a hotel. The flights with EgyptAir came in at £300 each, which was great news as it was well within their budget. He also got details on a mid-range hotel. It was only when she asked if he wanted to book it that he realised it might not be Cairo they wanted to go after all! So, he took the details and left it that he would return next week when he was a bit surer of what he wanted.

There was also another problem. The gulf war had only finished earlier in the year and trips to the Middle East were not recommended by the government. Although Egypt was some way from Kuwait, where the action had taken place, they were one of the biggest allies involved and, therefore, terrorist attacks couldn't be ruled out. Travelling to Egypt wasn't forbidden, it just wasn't recommended and, therefore, if the boys were going to go, they would be going against this travel advice.

The Friday night planning meeting went well although the boys found that travelling to this part of the world was much more complicated than they thought it would be. The travel agents had updated Glenn on everything they would need to do. They needed to go and get a number of injections, they had to get visas and Egyptian money. He had been advised to take a lot of shiny pound coins as these went down well with the locals for tips, etc. So, they had decided to take a bag of fifty £1 coins and £500 in cash as well as £1000 worth of the Egyptian pounds. They also needed to sort things out at work and book a week's leave each, so they set the date of departure as Saturday 30th November 1991.

Dad took them to the airport and pulled up in the drop off zone and they all climbed out and took the two suitcases out of the boot. He reached out and shook their hands. "Now, boys, look after yourselves, trust no one and stick together. You know I think this is a mad adventure and I can't see anything good coming from it. I mean two young lads on a treasure hunt into Egypt is just ridiculous. It will be one of your Granddad's last wind-ups I bet you," he said.

Ever the optimist, thought Brian.

"Yeah, no worries, Dad, who gets to go on an all-expenses paid trip to Egypt at our age. Might never get the chance to do something like this again. And even if it is a wind up, we get a week in Egypt and might even get time to see a pyramid or two which sounds spot on to me," said Glenn.

"I also don't like the idea of you carrying all that cash around with you. You should have got travellers' cheques and then you can get your money back if you lose them."

"Dad," said Brian, "no one gets travellers' cheques anymore. We have spread the money around in all our pockets and some in the suitcase and we have the credit card as a back-up. Stop fretting it will be fine."

"We will try and ring you every day, so you know we are OK," said Glenn.

"All right, well good luck then and see you in a week or so."

And with that, Dad climbed back in the car and the boys watched him go before turning into the departures entrance and the start of their adventure to Egypt!

155

Chapter 28

Egypt November 1991

The flight had been uneventful until the descent and the excitement of the geography the boys could see out of the window. The thing that amazed them was the complete lack of greenery. When taking off from Britain, the first thing anyone notice as soon as you climbed into the sky the overwhelming site of the landscape was how green it was. There was none of that here, but the immense oceans of sand. It was a fantastic sight and unlike nothing they had seen before. As they approached the city, Glenn said, "Look at that, Brian, three pyramids. I never thought they were so close to the city."

"It is amazing, that is some sight. Look at the little one, I wonder why that's so small," said Brian.

There were three pyramids in total but one of them as Brian had commented was a lot smaller than the other two.

"Must be a less important king or queen I guess."

"Were they all kings and queens then? To be honest, I have no idea, just presumed they were."

"I thought so. I thought that was the point of them. Bury them all with their valuables ready for the afterlife. It's a heck of a sight though, isn't it?"

"Yeah better make the most of it as I don't think we will have anytime for sightseeing on this trip. We can at least say we saw the pyramids though. What did you buy in duty free by the way?"

"Couple of bottles of Bells Whiskey in memory of Granddad!"

"Oh! I can't stand the stuff."

"It's not my favourite either, but I believe it's hard to get an alcoholic drink out here except maybe in the hotel, so if we are planning a celebration on a successful mission, it will have to be Bell's Whiskey I'm afraid."

"Great! Let's not start celebrating just yet though, eh?" said Brian.

The huge sprawling city of Cairo came into better view. Again, it was so different from back home. It was a sea of grey and brown buildings as far as the eye could see. They weren't skyscrapers, but they did all seem to be multi-floor high. The descent continued and it was clear to see the airport would be some way from the city so they would have to get transport back into the city centre and the hotel. The details they had were that it would be an eleven-mile journey and they had been advised to go to the bus station rather than a random taxi – apparently, they had minibuses running into the city on a regular basis.

They made it through the chaos of security and the visa process to baggage reclaim. They had both laughed and accepted in the chaos that their suitcases wouldn't arrive and be lost somewhere in Africa. They were therefore pleasantly surprised when they came around the carousel.

They followed the signs for the bus station amazed at the buzz and excitement all around them. It was an electric atmosphere. What an experience already. The other surprise was the weather. It was warm but they had expected an inferno, especially reading the tales from Granddad. The temperature display though in the terminal was reading 23 degrees. Sure, it was a lot warmer than the 9 degrees at home, but still came as a nice surprise.

They arrived at the bus station and got talking to a bus driver, who said he was the man to take them to the hotel and yes, he knew where the Grand Palace Hotel was. He took them across to his dodgy looking bus that already looked full of passengers. They climbed aboard and made their way to the only two seats at the back of the bus. They had to laugh when their cases were passed to them through the missing windows and had to put their backs to the crammed in cases behind them to stop them toppling into the bus. Brian looked at Glenn with a huge smile across his face. "This is crazy! Just what I expected though."

"Well, I think we are certainly getting the full Egyptian experience," replied Glenn.

The smiles disappeared though when they set off at great speed. At first, the roads were extremely wide, wider than the motorways at home and didn't have much traffic on them so they made good progress. However, when they hit the city proper, the roads became chaotic. There were no road markings and it seemed to be every man for themselves. The other alarming feature seemed to be that there were as many people on the roads as cars! Crossing roads here was a very dangerous occupation but the people looked nonchalantly accustomed to it. Life revolved around the roads with market stalls lining most of them.

As they pulled up at a junction, a man leapt out trying to sell them something which must have been food. They didn't recognise what the guy was trying to sell but he was persistent, walking along next to the minibus as it slowly made its way around the junction. Eventually he gave up. "What a way to make a living," said Glenn.

Eventually, they arrived at the hotel. It was a fantastic relief to get off that bus with their suitcases and bodies intact. To be fair to the driver, he had delivered on his promise to get them to their hotel. They paid him, picked up their cases and strolled into the hotel lobby. There were people everywhere and the place was roasting. The surprise at the discovery of the warm weather rather than desert heat was short lived. They had been sweating in the cramped conditions on the bus and the temperature wasn't much better in here. There appeared to be a congested maul, rather than a queue they would have found in Britain, around the reception desk. "Brian, I'll do the queuing, mate, to get us booked in if you go and see if you can find us something to drink, I'm gasping mate," said Glenn.

"OK. Not sure who's got the best deal here but will see what I can do."

Brian returned ten minutes later with two bottles of water just as Glenn had the attention of the receptionist. Checking in was a lot easier than they thought. They had to leave the passports with them overnight to collect the following day but were issued with a key and off they went to find their budget twin room with its own bathroom! Remembering the tip with the shiny pound coins, Glenn tipped the porter with one who looked well pleased with it and marched off with lots of "thank you, sir" comments. They both flopped on a bed and let out a huge sigh.

"Wow, what a day that was and we have only just arrived. What time is it, mate?" said Brian.

"Just on four pm, bro. Time to put our feet up for a couple of hours. I suggest we go to the hotel restaurant tonight, keep it simple and plan out tomorrow."

"Yeah, agree with that. The restaurant looks OK actually, that's where I got the water from."

They lounged around and unpacked and noticed just after five pm, it went dark. "Need to remember that Glenn when we are out and about, it goes dark fast and early round here," said Brian.

"I know. We don't want to get ourselves stuck on top of that mountain when the light goes out. Wouldn't fancy a night up there in the dark wilderness."

The restaurant was great, and they even managed to score a few bottles of Stella. Not their normal drink but it was alcohol and that would do the job and hopefully help them get some sleep. The plan they agreed on was simple. They needed to find somewhere to buy supplies for their trip out to the mountain. They had their map but needed food, drink and some blankets just in case they did get stranded out in the dark.

The also needed a couple of powerful torches and find out where they could hire a car for a few days. Mind you, after the journey in from the airport, they were not looking forward to the drive. As they pointed out though as soon as they could get out of the city, the roads looked easily navigable. It was getting out of the city that would be the issue.

And some digging tools, spade, pickaxe something like that if there was indeed some treasure to dig up at the end of this journey.

They were tucked up in bed by ten pm, happy with their plan for the following day. It had been all the experience they had hoped for and so much more, and it was only day one.

And the plan went as scheduled. Everything procured including renting a small four-door Renault for the week. It was after lunch when they returned to the hotel. Too late to set off today, so they spent another night in the hotel restaurant and another earlyish bedtime setting the alarm for eight am the following morning. Phase one of the adventure was completed and successful. Glenn could tick it off his to do list.

Thoughts were hugely positive. Roll-on tomorrow as the light went out.

Chapter 29

They ate a hearty breakfast in the hotel, conscious that it could be their last really good meal for a while. It was about nine am when they got to the Renault parked in the multi-storey car park. They opened the boot, not much room for much more than the supplies they had to fill it. "Hope this treasure box ain't huge," commented Brian. "We will never get it in here."

"I know I was thinking the same thing. I reckon we may have slipped up ordering this car. I think you were right, we should have gone for the expensive jeeps. I mean we have the dosh, don't we? I just thought a little Renault was less conspicuous."

Brian was holding his hands up defensively, "Don't tell me, Brother, you're the bloody tight one with the cash. I told you we are going out in the desert and you might need something with a bit of power!"

"Yeah, but I got to drive round these roads first before we get anywhere near the desert and I just didn't fancy driving one of those big things around here. I would be pranging it all over the place."

"Exciting though, isn't it? At last to be getting out there and seeing if we can find this box. I mean we have to be realistic it was what, nearly fifty years ago when they stashed it and it was in the middle of a war. I can't see it being there but at least we can say we came, and we gave it a go."

"Yeah, but will we conquer? I would be happy if the manuscript rang true and we could follow it all the way even if someone had beaten us to it."

They set off out of the car park and into the bustling street. They both fancied themselves as good map readers, but Brian took the first stint as Glenn drove. "Jesus, look at this lot," he said as he edged his was out slowly into the traffic.

It took them over ninety minutes of very stressful encounters and a few crossed words before they eventually found their way out of Cairo and, they thought, heading west towards El Alamein. It wasn't as free flowing as they remembered from the journey from the airport, and the wider roads just meant the cars were all going a breakneck speed. It was very nerve wracking, terrifying in some places but eventually they settled in and got used to the driving conditions. After a further two hours, they pulled over in a town called Damanhur and took out the maps.

"I think we took the wrong road out of Cairo, Glenn. Look here on the map, if we are in Damanhur, we are taking the long way around. Its 12:30 already and I reckon we have still got another hundred miles to go."

"OK, no worries, we live and learn. Let's have lunch on the go. Do you fancy doing an hour or so and I will have a look at the map?"

"Yeah, give us the keys."

It took them another two hours to reach the outskirts of El Alamein. Time to pull over and have another check of the map. They got out of the car and started stretching their limbs. They had been travelling in the little Renault for about five and a half hours already and the original thoughts, looking over the map the night before, was that they would be at the mountain in four hours.

"I'm worried, Brian," stated Glenn. "It's probably another hour to the mountain from El Alamein and its already gone half past two in the afternoon. We won't get there until near four and it goes dark just after five, remember."

"We have a decision to make then, don't we? As I see it, we have two options. We either carry on, find the mountain and have a little search today but all the while knowing we will have to stay over in the car out in the desert, or, we head back to the hotel the quicker route, the route we should have come on in the first place, and start again tomorrow."

"Well, I favour the second option. It feels a bit crap, but we have got all week so plenty of time. Plus, we can follow this road back to Cairo," Glenn said, tracing his finger down the map. "Which, as you say, we should have come down, and it will give us both some experience of the road and more accurate timings. I reckon if we try it again tomorrow, we can easily get here earlier in the day."

"We also need to get our backsides out of bed at sunrise and head straight out. We wasted three or four hours before we even got out of the city."

"You're not wrong there, mate. OK, it's settled then. Right, according to the map, we need to head south and pick up the Mehwar El Dabaa Road, which takes us straight back to Cairo. We will be back early evening and hopefully not too much driving in the dark. I guess I am taking the next stint behind the wheel?"

"Nice one, Glenn," said Brian, tossing Glenn the keys.

It actually took them less than three hours to get back to Cairo and a further hour to navigate the city centre back to the hotel. Better than that morning; however, they had basically spent nine hours driving around in a huge circle and achieved absolutely nothing. They were tired and dejected as they got ready to go out for something to eat. The hotel porter had recommended a restaurant that was about a four-minute walk away and would give them the authentic Egyptian experience.

Chapter 30

They arrived at the Koshari al-Tahrir just before eight pm and took a table for two by the window. The waiter handed them a menu and the boys looked it over. "Would you like me to recommend something for you, gentlemen?" said the waiter, who had noticed they were struggling.

"That would be great," said Glenn. "Thank you."

"OK, sir, I would recommend the house special – a Koshari. It's very nice. It has rice, macaroni, onions and garlic juice. Very, very nice."

"OK, two of those please," said Glenn. "Do you have any beers on the menu?"

"Sorry, sir; no, we don't have beer."

"OK, a jug of water then please," said Glenn, handing the menus back to the waiter.

"No beer," grumbled Brian. "After the day we have had, I could have drunk a bucket."

The meal was delicious and didn't disappoint. If they got the chance, they vowed they would come back and try something else from the menu. "I don't fancy sitting here drinking water. We will have to go back to the hotel," said Glenn.

"We passed a café that looked pretty good on the way. Why don't we try in there first and we always have the hotel to fall back on?"

"Sounds like a plan."

They paid the bill, again leaving a tip and headed off to the café. The streets again were alive with people creating a vibrant atmosphere. They entered the café which was crowded and tightly packed and grabbed a table for two. Unfortunately, there was no beer to be had there but they ordered two coffees and some rather nice-looking cakes.

"Well, that was a waste of a day," said Glenn. "I can't bear the thought of spending another nine hours in that car tomorrow, getting lost around Egypt."

"I know. What we really need is kind of local guide or someone who could at least get us out of the city in one piece and a damn site quicker than we have been managing."

"Hello, English," said a man sat next to them on the next table. He sat alone but was literally pushed up against the boys table. "How are you enjoying our beautiful country?"

"It's an exciting place if a bit chaotic, especially when driving," said Glenn.

"Oh no, you don't want to be driving on the roads here. Takes practice and experience – not a place for you English."

"That's just what we were saying," said Brian. "We could do with someone who could drive us around and knew what they were doing."

"That's me, I am guide. I can take you anywhere you want to go in Cairo. This is my beautiful city. Let me introduce myself, I am Khaled El Kedwany," said the Egyptian, bowing to the boys.

"That's great, Khaled, nice to meet you. I am Glenn and this is my brother, Brian," said Glenn, shaking Khaled's hand.

"OK, English, get the coffee and tell me how I can be of service to you."

Brian ordered some more coffee as Khaled joined them on their table. He was probably a bit older than the boys, good looking with a healthy growth of stubble on his chin. He went on to tell them he lived on his own in Cairo since his parents passed away a few years ago. He said he was indeed a guide who worked with lots of the hotels around here, showing tourists around the city.

It was only then that Glenn thought they could have got a guide through the hotel porter. Having said that though, was it exactly legal what they were up to? They weren't sure. Better to use this guy, get the treasure, pay him a few gold coins and back to the hotel no questions asked.

169

"So that is enough about me what about you, English, where are you from in England?" asked Khaled.

"Just outside Manchester," said Glenn.

"Ah Manchester United. Great club, Alex Ferguson. Do you go to Old Trafford? That is my dream to go and watch United there. They call it the theatre of dreams! Fantastic."

"Bloody hell," said Brian. "There is more to Manchester than bloody Manchester United. We can't stand them, to be honest."

"Ah, you are Manchester City then. You are blue not red."

"No, not them either. We support a small club called Oldham Athletic. We're sick of the Manchester clubs, everyone supports them where we live, and we get it rammed down our throats."

"AHHH, Oldham Athletic; yes, I know them, Joe Royle. They are in the first division and played at Wembley last year – very unlucky to lose."

"Yes, that's it, Khaled, that is a surprise. I wouldn't have thought someone in Egypt would have heard about Oldham," said Glenn.

"Oh yes, we see all the English football over here. I love watching English football."

"All right, nice one," said Brian.

"So how can Khaled be of assistance to you. Where is it you are looking for?"

"We are looking to make a trip out to Mount Himeimat. We are following in the footsteps of our Granddad from the war. He spent some time in that area between battles and on top of the mount in particular. We are hoping to go and collect something he left behind," said Brian.

"He left something behind from all that time ago?" asked Khaled.

"Memories. What Brian meant to say he left his memories there and he's asked us to go back and visit the place and take some pictures for him. Take them back to England to jog his memory," said Glenn, glaring at Brian.

"Yeah that's it, Khaled. We tried getting there yesterday but ended up doing nine hours in the car and never found it," said Brian.

"OK, I can get you there," said Khaled hesitantly. "But it's quite a drive out. Might be a two-day trip and we would have to stay over at the base of the mountain I would think."

"That's OK, we are happy to do that."

"Have you got a vehicle, or would you like me to hire you one?" asked Khaled.

"No, we are OK," said Glenn. "We have hired a car and it drove pretty well today so I think that will do us fine. How much would you charge us, Khaled?"

"Twenty English Pounds per day paid up front before we set off."

"OK, that's sounds reasonable to me. We were hoping to set off early tomorrow morning, does that work for you?"

"Sure thing, English, that's OK with me. Where are you staying?"

"We are in the Grand Palace Hotel."

"OK," said Khaled as he finished his coffee and got to his feet. "I will meet you outside the hotel at seven am."

"Oh, one other thing. We burned most of the petrol yesterday so we will need to fill the car up before we set out," said Glenn

"No problem, English, as long as you pay, I can do that," said Khaled raising his hat. "See you in the morning," and with that, he left.

"What do you think to that then? We got our guide, but can we trust him?" said Brian.

"He seems OK although he leapt on your comment about collecting something from the mountain."

"Yeah, I know I knew as soon as I said it, I shouldn't have."

"Well, it's done now. We are just a couple of normal blokes; he can't expect us to be up to no good. And let's face it, the chances of us finding something have to be slim."

"Well, we are buggered on one front. We said we were going to take pictures, but we haven't even got a camera. Let's just hope he is not too inquisitive and is happy enough with the forty quid just for chauffeuring us there and back."

"Yeah, fancy not bringing a camera that was a bit of an oversight although I know we didn't come here to sight see but it would have been a good cover story to go back with a few snaps at least."

"OK, let's get off back to the hotel; it's been a long day and I could just nail a couple of those pints of Stella before we go to bed."

"Great shout that, bro."

They paid the bill, including Khaled's, and made their way back to the hotel.

Chapter 31

They were up at just after six am but were too early for breakfast in the restaurant. For now, they would have to make do with the digestive biscuits they had brought along on the trip. They had crisps, chocolate and drinks in the back of the car for later in the day.

"You never know," said Glenn. "The petrol station might be like back home and you can get some hot food there. That will do us for our breakfast."

"I haven't specifically been looking but I don't think I have seen a petrol station. Presumably they exist all over the place. There are enough cars on the road for the demand."

"Let's hope so. OK, so the car is full of the supplies. We have our rucksacks here with a change of clothes and we have the blankets in the car if we need them."

"Yeah, I am just wondering what Khaled will be thinking when we go up the mountain with the small pickaxe and shovel we bought."

"Yeah and no camera! As you said last night, let's just hope he is happy enough with the forty quid not to ask too many questions."

"I have been thinking about that. What if we offer him another ten quid bonus to get us back to the hotel?"

"Well, I would hope that was already part of the deal, but I get where you are coming from. Fifty quid though that's quite a bit of dosh."

"Yeah, but let's face it, though, we tried it ourselves and made a right bugger of it. At least, this way we should make it there and back in one piece."

"Good point well made. I will put Khaled's fifty pounds in this pocket, and I have a further hundred in the other pocket, as well as about two hundred pounds worth of Egyptian money."

"And I have a further hundred then and I have about fifty in Egyptian money so we should be fine with that lot. I will lock the rest in the safe best not to have it all on us out there."

"Sounds like a plan. Right, I think we are ready to go. Let's hope he is here."

They made their way down the stairs and through the hotel lobby which was as quiet as it had been since they had been there. Out through the front doors and there was Khaled exactly as he said he would do. That was a promising start. He looked dressed and ready for the desert and carried a large rucksack on his back.

"Good morning, English, and what a beautiful morning it is," said Khaled.

"Morning, Khaled, great to see you. Are you ready for our adventure?"

"Yes, sir, lead the way and we can get moving before the rest of the city wakes up."

They made their way to the car park and opened the car, depositing their rucksacks in the back. Khaled didn't look too impressed with their ride. "Is this it, English, we are going out into the desert you know. I thought we would be travelling in style."

"We got a good price on this and the petrol consumption is pretty good," said Glenn.

Brian was laughing out loud. "You will do for me. Khaled. I have been telling him that, but he is too tight to part with his money or even Granddads, it's not even his."

"Sorry, I don't understand English. He doesn't have any money of his own?"

"No, it's OK, Khaled, ignore Brian. Our granddad paid for our trip so really, we are spending his money. Talking of money, here is your forty pounds as agreed for the two-day trip."

"Thank you. Would you like me to drive? I think that would be best."

"That would be perfect," said Glenn. "I think we had enough driving yesterday for any Englishman out here."

He passed the keys to Khaled and jumped in the passenger seat. Brian jumped in the back and Khaled started the engine. "On the subject of money, Khaled, we are really pleased you agreed to take us on our little journey and will throw in another ten pounds if you get us back to the hotel by tomorrow night. Deal?" said Glenn.

"Sounds good to me, English. You have a deal," said Khaled as he pulled the car out of the car park.

Straight away, his driving was far more confident than the boys and he was making progress through the traffic. He took a turning off the main road, took a few side streets and pulled up in a filling station. They refuelled but it didn't have any warm food as they had hoped only more local snacks and chocolate. They chose the chocolate which would be their staple diet for the next two days.

They were out of the city in around thirty minutes. Three times quicker than yesterday. They were heading west and recognised some of the features from their return journey last evening. To some extent, they could relax although you never felt completely safe on the roads. Just before eleven am, they passed the signs showing El Alamein north and turned south. In their mind, they knew they were only about thirty miles away from their destination, Mount Himeimat.

They stopped for a quick comfort break. As they did, another car drove past them and carried on down the road. "Did you see that jeep, Glenn? I am sure I saw the same one at the petrol station this morning. You don't think they could have been following us, do you?"

"What! Give over, Brian, who would possibly be following us out here? There are loads of jeeps like that, relax, mate."

"Guess you're right but I am bloody sure it was the same jeep, mate."

They set out again and scanned the horizon in front of them for the mountain. It reminded Glenn of a game they used to play as kids on a family day out to Blackpool. The winner was the one who spotted Blackpool tower first and Dad always made a big fuss of the winner. The idea was to beat Dad to it which of course he always let them win.

After about twenty minutes, they could make out the mountain on the horizon. They were glued to it as it got closer and closer. They felt like they already knew it although it seemed different than the explanation Victor had given. Brian raised the point and Glenn pointed out that was because they were approaching from the north not the south as Granddad had done.

They reached the base of the mountain around mid-day and pulled up. They piled out of the car and hit the food they had brought with them. Khaled started to set up a small portable stove he had brought in his rucksack, "I know you English like to drink tea all day so I have brought some along," he said.

"Spot on, Khaled. We don't do anything before we have had a brew," said Brian.

They sat down with Khaled and enjoyed lunch, looking up at the mountain. To this point, it had all been a story, something they had read from the memoirs of Granddad Victor, but now sat there looking at the mountain, it all seemed very real.

Chapter 32

They prepared to set off up the mountain. They donned their rucksacks and got the tools and bottles of water out of the boot of the car. "Planning on doing some digging while you are up there, English?" asked Khaled.

"Better to be prepared my dad always told me, Khaled, you never know what we will face when we get up there. We will be back before it gets dark so you can put your feet up for the afternoon," said Glenn.

"No worries, English. Good luck with your adventure," said Khaled as he made himself comfy in the shade of their vehicle. He tipped his hat over his eyes and looked like he was going to get some serious sleep in.

"OK, bro, let's do it," said Brian and they set off towards the gap between the small and large mountain as described in Granddad Victor's story.

"Remember, Brian, we are approaching from the north, so we have to try and reverse the instructions Granddad gave us.

I wrote them down so let me read them out again, so we are both sure what we are going to do."

"OK, I guess it won't harm going through it one more time," said Brian.

Glenn took the paper from his pocket and began to read out loud as they walked towards the mountain.

"We approached the mount from our base in the southwest, following a 45-degree path (not sure that's relevant but captured it anyway).

"When we reached the mount, we tracked the base of it east until we saw the little mount.

"Mount Himeimat is easily identified from its unique geological features. It consists of two mounts, a big and smaller one.

"Continue into the valley between the two mounts with the larger mount on your left-hand side.

"In the centre of the valley, there will be a rough path that makes the climb to the top easier. (there are a couple of other paths just inside the valley – ignore them and take the 3rd path) We didn't measure how far into the valley we walked but it looked halfway to both ends.

"Use the path to climb to the top of Mount Himeimat. It's quite steep in places and we found this difficult in the dark.

"Once on top, measure 120 paces in a west direction. That will give you the depth into the mount before turning north and walking to the rim of the mountaintop.

"From there, scramble down the side 14 feet to a ledge and then turn to your left.

"There are many small caves and ridges that run along here. I counted 23 paces on my way back from where we buried the treasure.

"There is a prominent rock next to it and you scratched a V on it Vic as a guide. The treasure was buried here in the small ridge in the face of the mountain."

Glenn finished and popped the paper back in his pocket. "OK, so we head into the valley and find the path. Unfortunately, Victor describes it as the third path into the valley but that's from the south," said Glenn.

"Is it actually Granddad describing it or his mate, Frank?"

"Does it matter?"

"I guess not. So, we either go right through the valley and then come back on ourselves or he also says it felt about halfway into the valley. If we see a path halfway in, then I reckon we take that."

"Agree with that, Brian, not sure we need to go all the way through and come back. Here is the valley, here we go!"

They started their way through the valley and found a path on their right up the mountain but that was nowhere near halfway through, so they decided to carry on. It didn't take long to find another path. "OK, let's take this one," said Glenn. "It looks about halfway through although further down, it looks like it comes back on itself. I'm wondering if we should go through to the south and start again."

"Nah, I reckon this is the one, mate, let's go for it."

They took the path and started to climb. It wasn't too difficult and like Victor had explained, they did have to clamber in a few places but on the majority of the path, they could walk it. As they got to the top, the first thing to hit you was the view. You could see for miles in every direction and it wasn't difficult to see why this was used as an advantage point in the war.

"Right, one hundred and twenty paces wasn't it, west?" said Brian.

"I have the compass here and that's west, mate," said Glenn, pointing the way. "You step out the paces and I will follow making sure we keep going west."

They did this carefully and then turned exactly north. "So we follow the compass exactly north until we reach the edge of the mountain," said Brian.

Again, they did this as precise as they could and probably took a lot more time over it as they needed but, excited as they were to get there, they decided to do the job properly. As they reached the edge, they had a drink break and peered down the side of the mountain.

"That doesn't look as easy as we have just come up, Brian."

"No, it bloody doesn't and how on earth did they do it with a box in the dark?"

"Well, let's give it a go just be careful."

They edged their way down, remembering they were looking for a ledge after about fourteen feet. After a minute or so of scrambling down, they unbelievably found a ledge of sorts and stood on it. "This has to be it," said Glenn. "What was the next part. Turn to your left and carry on a further twenty-three paces," he said, reading the instructions from the paper before returning it to his pocket. They moved along the ledge 23 paces and stopped and looked around.

"The instructions mention a big rock with a V on it. There are plenty of rocks but nothing you would remember as prominent I would say," said Brian.

"No, I can't see one either. We haven't passed one and there are none in the next 10 yards or so where it looks like the ledge finishes. OK, so let's search everywhere here and see if we can find anything."

They spent an hour looking everywhere. On hands and knees and rubbing their hands across the surface of the mountain. They even reverted to looking over the ledge and seeing if there was anything possible down there. The end of the ledge spelt the end as there was no way anyone could walk along there it was more of a cliff face. Certainly no one could have done that in the dark and it would have surely been in the instructions if they had.

They sat down in despair and covered in dust from scrambling around. The view out across the desert was sensational in the late afternoon sunshine. It was absolutely beautiful and yet seemed to spell the end of a huge wild goose chase. They simply sat there and didn't say anything for ages, letting the silence say everything they felt.

"Bollocks," said Glenn at last.

Brian was shaking his head, "No matter how unbelievable it seemed, I still thought we would find something up here." He threw a rock out off the mountain.

"So did I, mate. Gutted. Surely the old man wasn't winding us up. He truly believed the treasure was here. You could feel it from the words in his story."

"I think it is here but somehow we are looking in the wrong place."

"What now, do we give up? It's going to be dark in an hour and we don't want to be up here then?"

"We better make our way back to Khaled and the car. We could always try again tomorrow before we set off back."

"We could and I think we should, but this time go right through to the south and follow the instructions to the letter. If we don't find it, then no one can say we didn't try."

They trudged their way back the way they had come. The climb back to the top of the mountain was tough, especially with all their kit which they had brought down with them. It was going dark as they reached the car. Khaled was making some food on the stove when they arrived.

"Ah, English, how did it go, did you complete your adventure. Would your grandfather be pleased?"

"Yes, it was fantastic, Khaled, but we are going to go back in the morning," said Glenn. "We didn't quite find what we were looking for but now we have a better understanding of the terrain. We should be able to get up there and back by lunchtime."

"Good job, I brought lots of food then. It will be ready shortly."

"And I brought one of those bottles of Bells. I reckon we could just nail that."

"Now you're talking, Glenn, let's knock the top off that we have earned a drink," said Brian.

"Not for me, English," said Khaled, holding his hands up as if in surrender.

And with that, they settled down and watched the sunset which was spectacular here out in the desert. The food and the whiskey went down very well. Khaled had made himself a bed out there under the stars with a couple of blankets, but the boys decided to sleep in the car. It had been a long, and in the end, a very disappointing last few days. The whiskey had worked, and they were very sleepy.

"Just think, Brian, Granddad spent a few nights sleeping out here in the desert. What a beautiful place it is. The stars are amazing. I love looking up at the night sky and it doesn't get any better than in the desert," said Glenn.

All he heard back was some quiet snores as obviously Brian was out straight away. He pulled the blanket over him and settled down for a long overdue sleep. It can't have been a load of nonsense, could it?

Chapter 33

They woke just after seven which was a surprise as it had been light for over an hour. It just showed them how tired they were. They both climbed out of the car and spent five minutes stretching limbs and backs. Sleeping in a car in a desert was not something they would be recommending anytime soon.

Khaled was up and had lit the stove for a morning cup of coffee. Glenn walked about thirty yards away to go to the toilet. He stood there looking at the mount, shaking his head. He still couldn't believe they were out here looking for treasure. I wonder if it is up there and we just don't find it. Oh well, maybe that was for the best and the actual location will remain unknown forever.

He wandered back to the camp and Brian handed him a steaming mug of coffee. "Life saver, Brian; cheers, mate," he said.

"Morning, English," said Khaled. "Are you still planning on returning to the mountain today?"

"Yes, Khaled, we need to go back up the mountain this morning and have a look around."

"Would you like me to come with you? You are obviously looking for something you can't find, maybe I can help."

"No thanks, Khaled, it's something me and Brian should do together."

"OK, English, no problem. I will put some food on before you set out. It will take us most of the afternoon to get back to Cairo so it would be good if you can be back here for mid-day."

"Sure thing," said Brian. "I don't fancy spending hours up there again anyway."

They ate a kind of porridge Khaled had made and then set off following their route from the previous day back to the mount. This time though they made their way right through the valley to the south side and then turned back on themselves.

"Right, there are two things to follow in the instructions. One is that we should take the third path on our left and two it should be about halfway through the valley," said Glenn.

"OK, lead us out then," said Brian, gesturing to Glenn to set off.

They took it easy and found the first two paths clearly in the left-hand big mountain of the two. A little further along they came across the third path. "Right, there is the third path absolutely no doubt about it, it's very clear. The problem is its no way halfway through the valley more like a quarter or third," said Glenn.

"You're right, that is quite clearly the third path. So, it's either a new path that's appeared since Victor was here or he just measured out its location in the valley incorrectly. Easy thing to do in the dark I suppose."

"OK, so I say we take the path. If it turns out incorrect, we can always come back down and see if there is another path further along. But the description is quite clear it's the third path, so let's get climbing."

They climbed the path and it zig zagged its way up the side of the mountain until they came out on the top of the plateau. They took out the compass and pointed it west. Glenn stepped out steady paces until they reached one hundred and twenty and stopped. Brian took the reading for direct north and they followed this to the edge of the plateau at the north edge of the mountain.

"If you look where this has brought us out, I will say we must be fifty to sixty yards away from where we went over the side yesterday," said Brian.

"Yes, and if you look, there is even an easier path here that drops down," said Glenn. He couldn't hide the excitement in his voice that following the instructions from the south had brought them to a different point. This could be a good omen.

"We are looking for a ledge after about fourteen feet. Come on let's move on."

"Should we leave our rucksacks up here as it was a real pain dragging them down there yesterday?"

"Good idea. Grab the tools and a bottle of water and leave this lot up here. Come on."

They left their rucksacks at the top and scrambled down the path until it came out on a ledge running off in both directions. There were a number of small caves cut into the rockface.

"This looks a lot more promising, Glenn."

"It does, doesn't it. Right, we need to turn to our left, east, and pace out twenty-three paces. I will do it as the paces I took on top seem now to be more accurate."

They made their way along the ledge. Glenn counting out loud each step he made. They stopped at twenty-three looking around them at all the geological features.

"OK, there are a number of rocks and caves, but that rock I would say would be the most prominent if I was looking at this scene fifty years ago," said Glenn, pointing to a rock in front. He bent down and started to rub his hands across the rock looking for the magical V sign Victor scratched on it.

"Can you see anything?"

"Not yet," he replied as he moved his way around the side of the rock between that and the face of the mountain. "Hang on, I have found something. There is definitely something here but it's hard to make out."

"Let me have a look," said Brian as he knelt down next to Glenn. He examined the face of the rock and could definitely feel something. He took the bottle of water out of one of his pockets and squirted water all over the face of the rock and then rubbed it with his hand. "That's a bloody V, Glenn, I am sure of it."

"Scratched here fifty years ago by our Granddad. Well, I be damned," said Glenn who just sounded amazed that it was here. They both turned around to the face of the mount and looked at the base of the mountain and the path. "It has to be here that they buried it although there is nothing obvious to me."

They took out the tools and started probing the ground. Sometimes clanging off rock but sometimes getting purchase and digging out the earth, stone and sand that had been here for half a century. They were digging and searching for only about ten minutes when Brian announced, "I think I have got something. This is the only place where the ground is soft enough for two or three feet. This has to be it."

"Dig out as much as you can."

Brian started digging and had dug out eight shovels worth when he hit something. He looked at Glenn who was wiping the sweat from his forehead. He nodded back to Brian to carry on. He shovelled out a few more before it became too difficult to get into the space. He reverted to digging out handfuls and slowly revealed a container. Once he could get right around it, he grabbed both ends and pulled it out and sat it on the floor between them. Glenn remembered the description his Granddad had written the first time he had seen this box in the German jeep:

Franky was trying to force open the top of a can about a two-foot-long and a foot high. Looked like an old ammunition tin I was thinking but it was pretty heavy, so there was something in it. The top came off and Franky let out a whistle, which wasn't the easiest of things to do out here in this dry desert with dry lips.

"Well, that's a tin about two-foot-long and a foot-high."

"I know." Brian took out his screwdriver and started to prize off the lid. He slid it around the seal loosening the top. He put down the screwdriver and grabbed the top firmly pulling it off the container. They both looked in and just stared for what seemed like a lifetime. The bright gold flashes of the contents of the box were almost hypnotic.

"Would you look at that beautiful sight," said Glenn.

"Amazing, I just cannot believe that. It's astonishing!"

They both grabbed a hand full of coins letting them slip through their fingers back into the box. Glenn took out one of the coins and had a closer look at it. Victor was right, they looked anciently old. They were round shaped but very uneven not like modern coins that were exactly round. On one side, he saw what looked like a warrior with possible a spear and a bow and arrow. He couldn't really make anything out on the reverse side. He looked at another one and that was very similar although not identical. Probably an indication that the coins had been hand made a long time ago.

They sat on the ledge dangling their legs over with the box between them. Both boys were having a good drink of their water bottles. "OK, believe it or not, that might be the easy part of this adventure, Brian. We got to get those coins back to the hotel, into our luggage and back to the UK. And if we manage all that, then decide what on earth we are going to do with them," said Glenn.

"Before we go rushing off, Glenn, let's just saviour this a minute and think what we have done. We have followed a fifty-year-old treasure map into the middle of the desert and found gold. It's incredible, mate."

"I know."

They sat there in their own thoughts for a while. Eventually Brian scrambled to his feet, "All right, let's get going. What are we going to say if Khaled asked what we have here?"

"We'll just have to say it's a few souvenirs from the war our Granddad left behind. The box looks like it belongs from the war years. He's a good lad no reason for him to ask any more questions."

"No mention of gold then!" said Brian, grinning.

"No, Brian, no mention of gold hey."

They made their way back to the top of the plateaux and collected the discarded rucksacks from earlier. Brian carried the box. Although it was heavy, it wasn't a two-man job, and they made their way across the top of the plateaux before heading east and finding the top of the path they had come up earlier that morning. The climb down wasn't too bad. At the bottom, Brian handed the box to Glenn and they marched their way out of the valley over to the car, the camp and Khaled.

Chapter 34

Khaled was waiting to greet them and noticed the box immediately. He didn't take his eyes off it. "Ah, English, you have returned and looks like you found what you were looking for," he indicated the box.

"Yes, Khaled, it's some old souvenirs our Granddad left us from the war," said Glenn.

"Looks pretty heavy to me," he replied.

"It is a bit. I will put it in the boot of the car. Can we pack up camp and we can make our way back to the hotel now and try and get back in time for a decent meal?" said Glenn.

Both Glenn and Brian made their way around the back of the car and opened the boot. They sensed Khaled following them round. They wedged the box into a safe place in the boot so it wouldn't rattle around. Just then they heard a click and turned around. Khaled had a gun! And he was pointing it at the them.

"What the hell are you doing?" said Brian as both boys raised their hands in an involuntary movement. Probably the first thing anyone would do when someone was pointing a gun at them. They had never seen a real-life gun before just what you would see on TV or in the movies.

"Unfortunately for you boys, I heard you talking about the gold. It's obvious it's not your gold and I figured I would be taking this back to Cairo with me," said Khaled.

"And what about us, are you going to shoot us?" asked Brian. He wouldn't admit it but there was a quiver in his voice and who could blame him thought Glenn. This is a dangerous situation. Dad had said they were mad coming out here to a country they didn't know looking for treasure. He said it would be dangerous, but they hadn't really thought they would come across anyone who knew what they were up to. Khaled seemed a nice guy and they had trusted him. How stupid was that now!

"I'm not a killer, English. I figured I would leave you here and take the car back to Cairo. You may get out of the desert and if you did, then that's great. I like you two, but I would be long gone, and you wouldn't be seeing me again. I figure you can't exactly go to the police with this so you will just have to go back to England and regret the mistake of hiring me as your guide."

"You bastard," said Brian. "Our Granddad and his mates nearly died fighting to keep the Nazis out of your country. In fact, one of them did and now your stealing their inheritance."

"I'm not stealing anything, English. That was years ago. I am just making the most of a fortunate situation that has come my way."

The boys still with their hands in the air started to split and move around Khaled. Just trying to create two targets rather than one.

"Now don't do anything stupid, boys. I like you, but I will use the gun if I have too," Khaled said in a confident and sure of himself tone.

"No, you won't, Khaled, you have never fired a gun no more than I have," said Brian, moving in close to Khaled.

Khaled wheeled round and cracked the gun across Brian's chin knocking him to the ground. Glenn seized his chance and grabbed Khaled's arm that held the gun. The two of them struggled with each other trying to get the upper hand. They crashed about into the car. Khaled wrapped his leg around Glenn, and they plunged to the floor.

This was a fight to the death and Glenn was feeling the strength in Khaled. He hadn't looked too strong before but looks could be deceiving and he had a wiry strength about him. They continued rolling around the floor. Glenn was tiring and Khaled managed to force himself on top. His arm with the gun was down by his side and he tried to bring it up.

Glenn was resisting with everything he had left in him. Khaled's face was inches from Glenn. He could smell his sour breath and see the death intentions in his eyes. They both struggled with the gun as it came up to play a part in the fight. Both of them were grimacing with the pain of battle and both were as tired as hell. Glenn looked again into the eyes of Khaled and feared the worse.

Suddenly, there was a huge bang and Khaled headbutted Glenn on the nose and he must have blacked out. When he came too, he could feel the whole weight of Khaled on top of him. What had happened, he couldn't work it out. Had he been shot? His mouth was full of blood and he started to gag. He used whatever strength he had left to roll Khaled off him who was motionless. Glenn started spitting out blood into the sand. He was exhausted and just lay there perched on his arm trying to get his breath back.

After a few minutes, he regained a bit of strength and managed to sit up. His nose was bleeding. The headbutt from Khaled had bust his nose and that was the cause of the blood in his mouth. He had some tissues in his pocket and got them out and applied them to his nose trying to stop the blood. God that hurt. He then had chance to look around and survey the scene. Brian was sat propped up against the car looking out into space. He had the shovel in his right hand.

"What happened?" said Glenn.

"I killed him," said Brian, holding the shovel up that was covered in blood. "Looked like he was going to kill you so I just hit him as hard as I could. Made a bit of a mess."

"Jesus, I reckon you saved my life. How the hell did all this happen?"

They sat there for an age getting their breath back and in total shock. After a while, Glenn's nose stopped bleeding and he staggered to his feet. "Are you OK, Brian?"

"Yeah, just got a swollen mouth where he clobbered me with the gun, hurts like hell I can tell you. What about you, you OK?"

"I think so I can't feel any other damage than my nose. When you whacked him with that shovel, he gave me one hell of a headbutt on the nose. Must have blacked out as well. It's bloody sore but has stopped bleeding at least."

"Is he dead? I can't believe he isn't. I put everything I had into that swing."

Glenn walked across to Khaled's body and tried to get a pulse from his wrist. There was none. He was dead all right. He suddenly looked away from the body and threw up into the sand and sat back down.

They were silent for some time before they pulled themselves together. "What are we going to do now? We are stuck out in the desert with a dead body and a box of gold," said Glenn.

"I don't know I guess we will just have to leave him here and hope no one discovers him until we can make our escape. There hasn't been many people around while we have been here."

They stood around thinking about their next move. Glenn had an idea, "What about if we take the body back up on the mountain and bury him where we found the gold. That was left undisturbed for half a century so there is no reason why Khaled's body wouldn't be either."

"OK, I see what you're thinking there. It certainly might buy us a few weeks until we can get back home and lie low for a bit although I am a murderer, Glenn. I killed a man, can you believe that?"

"It was definitely self-defence, mate. If you hadn't killed him, he would have killed us, that's for sure."

"He said he wouldn't. He said he was just going to leave us out here and make his escape."

"Not once the fight had started. It was either him or us. I tell you what as well, I don't fancy trying to explain that to the local police. The whole story of us being here no one would believe it. They would throw away the key on us, mate, or worse. I don't even know what their laws are here, but I bet there not as soft as in the UK."

"You're right, Glenn. We have no choice then but to bury the body and hope to get the hell out of Egypt. Puts a nasty taste though on the gold and all the excitement we were feeling an hour or so ago."

"We can drive the car over to the foot of the path and then go from there."

They both got a hold of Khaled's body and put him in the front seat careful not to get any blood from his head in the car. Glenn drove the car over to the path while Brian took the shovel and tried to erase every bit of evidence that a camp had been here. It took him about thirty minutes but all that was left was you could see where the sand had been disturbed. *That will have to do*, he thought. Perhaps it would all cover over after a few days with the sand blowing about. He went over to join Glenn at the path.

Chapter 35

The boys faced a heck of a task to retrace their steps up the mountain, across the plateau and down the other side to the spot where they found the gold. Walking it was bad enough but to do it carrying a body would be torture. However, the adrenaline was pumping and that would help a considerable bit. They also wouldn't take the back packs and just put a water bottle each in a pocket.

"OK, here we go," said Glenn. "This is going to be tough, but I don't see we have any other choice. We have plenty of time before dark so take your time and shout out if you need a rest."

"Will do. Luckily Khaled here wasn't too big a bloke. Ready when you are."

They had rigged up a stretcher with one of the blankets and took up the strain. Glenn lead the way up the path, and they made good progress before stopping after ten minutes. They swapped positions and Brian took the lead. They weren't sure if it was easier at the front or the back so decided to keep switching round just in case. They stumbled through some of the narrow passageways and up the steeper bits and took another rest after a further ten minutes.

"We couldn't have done this in the heat of the summer. The sweat is pouring off me," said Bryan as he was taking a drink.

"I know what you mean there. Come on, let's crack on," said Glenn lifting the stretcher again.

They had gone up another twenty yards or so when suddenly they heard a shout, "Khaled, ahlan." The boys froze where they were then it came again, "Khaled izayyak." And a moment later "Khaled" again as they could hear someone coming up the path.

"Jesus, someone has followed us," whispered Glenn as he put the stretcher down on the ground. Brian crouched down and moved back along the path to look around the corner. A shot rang out from their pursuer and ricocheted off the rock by Brian in a puff of smoke. He dived back around the rock and Glenn joined him.

"What the hell are we going to do now?" said Brian. "Did you bring Khaled's gun up with you?"

"Yep," Glenn pulled the gun from the waistband of his jeans and held it out in front as they both edged to the edge of the rock. They looked back down the path and another shot rang out. They ducked back to safety." There is two of us against one of him and we both have a gun."

"Glenn, we are two kids from Oldham, we are not gun slingers. This guy might be an experienced kickass assassin, mate."

"And there's nothing I can do about that, Brian; we are fighting for our life here. Think, what can we do? We have the advantage of higher ground and in numbers."

"Jesus, I can't think I don't know this is turning out to be a bloody nightmare."

They stood there crouched down in silence. Since their pursuer had seen them, it didn't sound like he was coming up the path. He too was probably stuck in several minds on what to do next. "Khaled izayyak," they heard again.

"Right this is what we are going to do," said Glenn. "You take the gun and hold him off here. I will crawl around the side of the mountain, it's not too steep, and try and get either behind or on top of him."

"What you going to do then, jump on him?"

"I don't know I will see if anything occurs when I can get a better site of him. Wait till I start crawling off and let off a shot down the path. Remember though, I will be crawling there so be bloody careful where you are shooting. When I make my move, I will shout so as soon as you hear me, come charging down the path. If we attack him from both sides, we should be able to overpower him."

"As long as we don't take a bullet while we are doing this charging!" said Brian.

"You got any better suggestions, then I am all ears?"

"No, it's the best we have. OK, get going."

Glenn started to climb the rock and move out across the mountain but was hidden from the path by the walls in which his enemy was hiding.

Brian said to himself, "Let a shot off. I have never fired a gun in my life who does he think I am?" He heard Glenn move off and then edged around the corner and fired the gun. It was extremely loud in the confines of the path, louder than he was expecting and his ears were ringing with the bang. He ducked back and held his breath listening out for any movement.

Glenn had made his way out about ten feet from the path and was working his way down the mountain when he heard the shot. He stopped and listened for any movement but didn't hear anything. He was trying to work out how far down he would have to go. When they caught a glimpse of the guy from the path, he was only about twenty feet away. If Brian's shot had kept him in his position, he shouldn't be too far now.

He moved down about another fifteen feet and stopped again to get his breath and listen again for movement. Nothing. So, he started to move across slowly to where he expected the path to be. As he moved stealthily to the edge of the path, another couple of shots rang out. The first he presumed was Brian as it was further away. The second sounded literally just in front of him. If he wasn't careful, bloody Brian would shoot him!

He looked over the edge and saw the guy about four feet below him and six feet to his right crouched down behind his own rock for protection. If he had had the gun, he could easily have shot him right there. He had the element of surprise as the guys attention was firmly in front of him, looking up the path. He looked around him holding his breath with tension. What was he going to do?

There was a hefty rock on the ground next to him. That could be a good weapon. He picked it up as quietly as he could with both hands. He slowly raised himself but not quietly enough as the enemy heard the movement and swivelled round. Glenn saw the surprise in his face as he was so close. He hurled the rock with all his might and hit the floor. A shot rang out. He scrambled to his feet and dived over the edge to where the guy had been. "BRIAN!!!" he screamed.

He landed on his feet ready to fight but the rock had landed square across the skull of his enemy who now lay prone on the ground with the smoking gun still in his left hand. Brian came barrelling around the corner, gun in hand, and skidded to a stop. They looked at each other and then down to the corpse on the floor. He bent down and tried to feel for a pulse.

"You've killed him, Glenn."

"Oh god no, what have we got involved in here?" He sat down on his back side with his head in his hands. They now had two bodies to deal with. How were they going to get out of this one?

Chapter 36

After a few minutes of silence, Brian said, "I told you yesterday I thought someone had followed us, didn't I?"

"You did. Good observation that, mate. What we going to do now? We have two bodies and I just can't see how we get away with this."

"Well, at least you killed the second guy whoever he is. I know it's no consolation to you, mate, but that makes me feel a lot better after what I did to poor Khaled."

"Poor Khaled! It's his bloody fault we are in this mess."

"The first thing we need to do is find where this guy's car is. We better make sure he is on his own."

"I guess he must have left it round the south side of the mount, we wouldn't have seen him there. He could have talked to Khaled on mobiles all yesterday so would have known what was going on. We can't bury two of them, can we?"

"I doubt it. We need to think of something else. Whatever we do, we need to leave their guns with them, if they are found it might look like some kind of gang bust up. I am not sure how common guns are over here so perhaps only the baddies carry them. Might mean the cops don't look into the deaths too deeply."

"This is gruesome stuff. How are we going to live with ourselves after this fiasco?"

"As you said earlier, we were fighting for our lives. These guys wanted to rob us and leave us for dead. They got what they deserved and rather them than us is my feelings on the matter."

"If you put it that way, you have a point."

"Too damn right I do, Glenn," said Brian. "As I see it, we have to make it look like a local gang hit. Let's get the car, put all the evidence, bodies and guns in it I and burn it out. Meanwhile we get the hell out of here and back to Cairo as quick as we can."

"Well, it's a bit of a gory plan but I guess it's a plan. I presume you have never burnt a car out before and I bet it's not as easy as you think," said Glenn thinking through Brian's suggestion. "OK, let's do it. I will take a gun and go look for the other car while you drag the two bodies back down the slope. I will meet you back there as quick as I can," said Glenn.

"Oh great, I get the dead bodies, bloody marvellous plan that, mate."

"Stop moaning. I will be back as soon as I can."

Glenn set off down the path, off the mountain and took a right at the bottom to head south through the valley the way they had gone only a few hours ago that morning. *A few hours,* thought Glenn, *it felt more like days after what's just happened.* He concentrated on what he was doing, gun outstretched, as he reached the end of the valley and came out onto the south side of the mount. He looked in both directions but couldn't see another vehicle so set off walking around the bigger mount first.

He had gone a couple of hundred yards when sure enough he spotted a jeep up ahead. He cautiously approached in case there was a third member of the team, but the jeep looked empty. As he walked up to it, he realised he hadn't checked the dead guy for the keys. There was no one around and no sign of anyone. The keys luckily were in the ignition, which was a relief and what looked like a small campsite packed up in the back. He climbed in and drove it back to his meeting point with Brian.

Brian was already there with the two bodies lay on the ground. It was obviously easier dragging the bodies down the slope than it was carrying Khaled up earlier. Glenn pulled up and got out of the jeep and Brian offered him a bottle of water he was drinking from. "Cheers. So, have you worked out how we burn a car out then?" he said.

"No, I was hoping there would be some extra fuel cans on board that we could splash around."

"That's what I thought but there isn't."

"The only thing I can think of is to try and bust open the fuel tank then and try and spread the fuel around. Khaled had the matches, so we are sorted on the point of getting a light."

"All right, let's give it a go," said Glenn.

The boys had a look round the jeep, found the fuel tank but it was difficult to get at. Their idea was to give it a few whacks with the pickaxe to bust it open, but they just couldn't get at it. Brian weighed up the issue and came to the conclusion that the only hope was to tip the whole jeep over. He shared his view with Glenn who gave him the thumbs up to give it a go.

He jumped into the driver's seat and drove sideways at the mount. As it started up the face, he turned the wheel sharply, it passed the tipping point and over it went.

Brian climbed out. "Jesus, I hurt my bloody arm there, it's a good job I remembered the seatbelt," he said but at least he had set up a car accident scene.

They then had the gruesome task of disposing of the evidence. They set the scene with the two bodies in it, all their belongings from the two cars and the guns. They then set to work with the pick on the fuel tank and soon burst it open. Brian lit a match and the whole thing went up.

"That's our cue, let's get the hell out of here," said Glenn.

They jumped in the Renault and set off north. It was about four pm in the evening by then, so they had a good hour daylight to get as far away as they could. As the light was just going, they hit the main road and soon the nearest town. They pulled over to take stock of where they were. Looking at the map they had come out way further west than they would have wanted at a town called Ad Dab'ah.

"It looks about forty to fifty miles until we get to El Alamein. Not ideal that, Glenn," said a dejected Brian.

"No, not really. What do you want to do?"

"I reckon we give it a go in the dark," said Brian while he was studying the map. "It's probably a good four hours to get back to the hotel though, want me to take the first stint?"

"Yes," said Glenn wearily. His nose was still throbbing from the fight earlier. In fact, he ached everywhere.

They swapped seats and set off at a steady thirty-five to forty miles an hour. The road wasn't too bad at first until oncoming vehicles started to approach barrelling out of the darkness. That was nothing though to the ones that came flying up from behind, all high beams and horns, before taking over and cutting them up. As if they hadn't stretched their nerves and emotions to breaking point already that day, the six-hour drive was an absolute nightmare.

Eventually, they made it back to the hotel. They parked up, headed straight for their room, trying to be as anonymous as they could and literally crashed out from exhaustion. Not before though, stashing the gold under Glenn's bed and therefore bringing an end to the most incredible day of their lives so far!

Chapter 37

They didn't wake until almost eleven the following morning. Sheer exhaustion of the experiences the day before had just wiped them out. They slowly came around but didn't get out of bed other than a toilet break each. It was a very lazy start to their day.

"Looks like we made it out of there in one piece and it doesn't feel like someone is on our tail," said Brian.

"Well, let's not pat ourselves on the back just yet. We've been in here all night so no idea what's going on in the hotel."

"No, you're right. I keep expecting the police to burst in through the doors and take us off to some dodgy prison never to be seen again."

"Well, Mount Himeimat is a couple of hundred miles away. If they found those guys in the burnt-out jeep, surely it would still take them sometime to link it to two English guys based out of Cairo."

"So, what's the plan?"

"Well, we have two more nights booked in here before we fly back to Manchester. I say we keep a low profile. Stay in the room and order room service for two reasons: one so no one really remembers us if the police start asking questions and two because I don't want to let the gold out of our sight."

"The gold! Can you believe we actually found that?" Brian said shaking his head. "I'll put the do not disturb sign on the door. You get the gold out and let's have a good look at it."

Brian put the sign on the door, locked it and put the chain on just in case the police came bursting in. Not that it would stop them if they were determined but it made him feel better. Glenn had taken the box out from under the bed and started tipping the coins out across his bed. What a sight that was. All that gold glittering under the lights in the bedroom.

"Wow! It's the second time I have seen them, and it takes your breath away even more. We must be rich, mate, with that lot," said Brian.

"I guess we are, Brian, but we have to get them home first and then find a way of turning all this gold into cash we can spend. I don't fancy hiding it under the bed for the rest of my life and you can't exactly take one of these beauties down to the pub and open a tab with it."

"What will you do with your half of the money then?"

"Invest it in a new house and take a few years off work, that will do me nicely."

"Yeah I reckon Victor would have approved of that. I think I will do something similar but would like to throw a new car into that and a nice holiday somewhere. Somewhere not in the desert with guys shooting at me!"

"How's your conscience about killing those guys now?"

"I actually feel better about it. I guess you never get over it, but it was either us or them and I am happy with the outcome. The other thing I keep thinking is what Victor would have done if he had found himself in our position. And I am sure the answer would always be the same as our outcome. He, Franky and Micky fought for the gold in the first place just as we did."

"Well said, mate. Have you been practicing that speech? Let's count how many coins we have."

The smoothed out the duvet on Brian's bed and started to make piles of ten coins. In fact, over the next two days, they would do this several times.

"Three hundred and fifty-two," said Glenn.

"Yep one hundred and seventy-six coins each. Awesome. Well worth the trip."

"Worth killing two people for?"

"Listen, Glenn, we have to stop talking about that. We have to try and forget it and move on, otherwise it's going to eat us up."

"OK, point taken. Let's just not mention it again," said Glenn. "I have been thinking about our plan of laying low for a couple of days. I know I came up with it, but it would be far better if we got out and created ourselves an alibi or two. I mean a few pictures on day trips to the pyramids for instance. Everyone who visits Cairo visits the Pyramids whatever they are doing. It's just simply unexplainable if we didn't."

"Yeah, see where you are coming from but there is no way I am leaving the gold in the room while we go out and about."

"I know. The hotel books excursions out to the pyramids. We could book two tickets on one and just one of us go. The other can stay here with the gold and we just pretend they have been taken ill. Just a case then of buying a camera and taking loads of pictures. I will nip down to reception and see if we can book on to tomorrow's trip."

Chapter 38

Glenn returned about an hour later. "Blimey, Glenn, I thought you had got lost. To be honest, I started to think you had been nicked or something."

"Sorry, mate, it's just chaos down there getting something organised. Anyhow, I finally got two tickets booked on the excursion tomorrow. Sets off at eight am. We just need to decide who's going and who's minding the gold?" replied Glenn.

"Well, I don't mind going. I don't fancy spending two days stuck in this room even if it is with a pile of gold."

"All right, I'm happy with that. I will go out this afternoon then and see if I can buy a cheap camera and a couple of films."

"And a few bags of food. If we are going to hang out here for the next two days, we will need something to eat and drink rather than room service. We don't want anyone delivering stuff to the room while the gold is here."

"I am going to take a long hot bath first and then head out."

Glenn laid back in the boiling hot bath and relaxed into the bubbles as he discovered many bruises, aches and pains from the day before. He ran through the events again in his head. It felt like it had happened weeks ago rather than yesterday. Finding the gold had been an amazing thrill but the horrors of the fight and eventual murder of the two Egyptians brought panic back to him again. There was no suggestion of police in the hotel or anyone looking for the boys. He was certain they could never trace it back to them and certainly not in the couple of days before they left. Still it didn't stop the doubts and the panic.

Glenn headed out following the advice of the concierge as to where he could get the supplies he was looking for. He decided to buy three films for the camera and take a load of snaps while out and about in downtown Cairo. He even asked a couple of passers-by to take pictures with him in it and tried to take a picture of himself with landmarks in the background.

He bought loads of food, some he recognised and some he didn't and had to take a punt on. He returned to the hotel room and the boys ate a feast before getting another early night. Brian set his portable alarm clock for seven am and was up, showered and ready to go.

"I'm off, Glenn, be back late afternoon," he said.

Glenn didn't raise his head off the pillow just raised his right arm and gave Brian a thumbs up.

Brian had a great day. The pyramids were fascinating. He bought a few mementos to take back for the family and he followed the script and used up the two remaining films. He was gutted for Glenn as he had missed out, but it was sensible and the right thing to do for one of them to remain behind.

The boys were happy with the alibi they had created for themselves over those two days, following the return from the desert. Compared to that trip, the time spent in the hotel was very boring and very uneventful. It didn't stop their nerves jangling every time they heard someone on the landing outside the room though.

The time came for them to pack their cases and get ready to go to the airport. They felt that each half of the coins together weighed no more than two bags of sugar and spread around in the suitcases could easily be hidden. They took a few clothes out and left them in the bin and then spread the coins wrapped in underwear, socks, shirts and anything else they had.

Looking at both packed cases, they were happy they had done what they could. Now it was in the lap of the gods as to whether they would get through customs and back to Manchester. Checking in at the airport was extremely nerve-wrecking. They stood there while a very pleasant lady looked at their tickets and passports. They couldn't help looking around for police to come over and arrest them. Eventually, they got their boarding cards. The lady put a ticket on each of their cases and they disappeared on a carousel out the back.

Oh well, nothing they could do now. They either appeared in Manchester or they didn't. Security went to plan, and they found themselves on the plane. As soon as it left the ground, they both let out a huge sigh of relief. They were not home and dry yet, but at least it looked like they would make it home. If something bad was going to happen, it would happen on English soil and that gave them some confidence that it was going to work out OK.

Brian whispered to Glenn after a few hours flight time, "So what's the plan when we get home then?"

"I reckon we have to lay low for a few months. Stash the box at home and go back to work as if nothing has happened. If nothing has happened for a few months, then I reckon we start looking at how we sell it."

"That sounds like a plan to me. We have to play the long game here."

"OK, let's set a timescale and say if everything appears clear by Easter Sunday, we then make our next move."

"Deal," said Brian and settled back in his seat to try and enjoy the rest of the flight.

They touched down back in Manchester where it was raining. No surprise there. They had one more security gauntlet to run before they could get in Dad's car and feel a bit safer. Security went fine and they stood around the carousel waiting to see if the bags would come through. Loads of bags did before eventually Glenn shouted out, "There they are, Brian!"

"Easy, mate, it's just a couple of suitcases with dirty washing in remember."

Glenn realised his outburst and settled down, heart racing as the bags made their way towards them. They took them off and walked through 'Nothing to declare'. *Nothing to declare,* thought Glenn, *are you kidding me?*

They were out of the airport and across to the pickup point where Dad was waiting. He had a big beaming smile and the boys were so chuffed to see him, they flung their arms around them and shed a few tears.

"Hey there. Blimey, you have only been away a week calm down. Did you have a good trip?"

"It was a heck of a trip, Dad. Can we just go home please?"

"OK, no worries, jump in. Your mum's looking forward to seeing you."

Part 4
Easter Sunday 1992
Manchester

Chapter 39

It had been a quiet few months. No news at all from Egypt so that had to be good news for the boys. The coins had been stored in the bottom of the bedroom wardrobe at Glenn's and they had managed to mention it to no one. They had thought that was the best policy. The fewer people who knew about it the better and if it was only the pair of them nothing would get out. They had told family they had had a great trip to Egypt and visited all the places Granddad Victor had written about, but there was no treasure to be seen. Everyone believed them, why wouldn't they?

They were gathering at Mum and Dad's for the traditional Easter Sunday dinner. Glenn was pouring himself a beer in the kitchen when Brian walked in and closed the door behind him. "So, Easter Sunday is here. Our deadline for lying low and all seems well," he said.

"Yeah, all seems to be quiet, doesn't it? So, we need to think about what we do next."

"We need to sell the coins and think about how we spend it, that's what we do next."

"I know but where the hell do you start to sell something like that?"

"My first thought is one of the big museums, get a professor or curator, whatever they are called, to verify what we have and see if they will buy them or tell us how to sell them."

"Yes, that's when the secret is out, and I will feel exposed. But you are right, that's what we have to do. The only museums I know of would be the Natural History Museum or the British Museum, but they are in London."

"Do they do stuff like ancient Egyptian exhibitions, that kind of thing?"

"I've no idea but I am sure I have seen that they do in a movie I once saw. I think it's probably the best place to start."

"We need to ring them and ask a few questions first."

"It's easy enough to use the phones at work. I will ring directory enquiries in my lunch tomorrow – get a number and see if I can find someone we can talk too."

"OK, now the other thing I have been thinking is about Victor's manuscript. It's a fantastic story but it has Mount Himeimat written all over it. If someone reads that, they will know where the treasure was hidden and more importantly where we had to go and get it. If it then came out at that time two bodies were found there, they could definitely put two and two together and link it back to us."

"That's a really good point, Brian, what do you think we should do?"

"Have to burn the book, mate, what else can we do?"

"I can't bring myself to do that, Brian, it's his life's work. It's a great story and a part of history."

"That's all fine, mate, I understand that, but it might lead us to life in prison!"

"Mount Himeimat is only a small part of it. Let me take those bits out this week and just keep the battles and make out the treasure was lost. No one can then trace it back and we can keep the war stories. We are not going to publish them, only the two of us need to read them."

"Great, now pass me one of those beers," said Brian.

The following day, Glenn declined the invitation from the rest of the guys on the team to go for a pub lunch and stay at his desk. He had made a couple of sandwiches and ate them while he jotted down what he was going to do. He had decided not to mention the fact he had three hundred and fifty-two coins but that he had some and at this stage would only show one to whoever he found as an expert. He would say they had originated from Egypt and had been left to him by his Granddad. He knew the two most famous museums in London, so he was going to start with them.

He dialled directory enquiries and got the numbers for both. He decided to start with the Natural History Museum for no reason other than he had seen it in a crazy Disney film when he was a kid and had always wanted to go there ever since. He dialled the number and waited for an answer

"Hello," he said when it was answered. "I am looking for an expert in old rare gold coins."

"Rare coins," was the response. "What kind of rare coins?"

"I think they originate from Egypt and definitely look like they are made out of gold."

"Right, that sounds exciting but I'm afraid coins aren't really what we do at the Natural History Museum. We are more about animals, geography, space that kind of thing. You know natural history I suppose."

"Oh, right that's a shame. Do you have any ideas where I could get some help?"

"I am sure I don't know. I would probably try the British Museum if it was me."

"OK cheers, I will do that," and he replaced the receiver. *Of course, the Natural History Museum was about animals, plants and stuff like that. What an idiot. OK, let's try the British Museum.* He dialled the number which was answered straight away.

"Hi, I wonder if you could help me? I have some rare Egyptian gold coins and I was looking for an expert to have a look at them for me," he said.

"Ah you probably want to speak to Professor Montgomery then. I will put you through to his office." There was a click on the line. He thought this sounded positive. An angel of a voice came on the line next.

"Hello Professor Montgomery's office, how can I help you?"

"Hi there, you don't sound like an old professor, an expert in old rare coins. Well, certainly not what I was expecting."

There was a giggle at the other end of the phone. "I'm not. I'm Amelia, his secretary."

"Right," said Glenn. "I nearly jumped straight on the next train to London as soon as I heard your voice."

"You're a right charmer, aren't you Mr…" said Amelia.

"Mr Mulligan. Glenn Mulligan."

"OK, Mr Glenn Mulligan, how can the professor help you?"

"I have inherited some rare Egyptian Gold coins and I was looking for help in identifying exactly what they are and how I might go about selling them. If indeed I was going to sell them," he added quickly as he didn't want to be seen too keen to go straight into the sell even if this was only his secretary. "Actually, I don't know they are Egyptian or in fact if they are rare, but they definitely look like gold."

There was another giggle over the phone "Are you sure they are coins?" she said, laughing.

Glenn laughed. "Yes, they are definitely gold coins, of some kind."

"Well, if they are you have come to the right place. Professor Montgomery is one of the leading experts on rare coins in the world. Also, we have the largest collection of Egyptian artefacts outside Egypt in our museum. You should bring them down to see him. Where are you in the country?"

"I am up in Manchester so it will be a bit of a trek. I probably need a couple of days to sort out my arrangements here. Could the professor see me on, say, Thursday and I will come down for a couple of days?"

"Two days in the smoke for a northerner, are you sure you can cope with that?"

"Yes, I think I can manage eating jellied eels and drinking horrible flat beer for a couple of days."

"I am sure you can, Mr Mulligan. The professor could see you at twelve noon on Thursday, how does that sound?"

"Sounds great and please call me Glenn. I don't suppose you fancy showing me the sights of London while I am down there?"

"Glenn, on a school night! We shall have to see. I will see you on Thursday at twelve noon in the meantime."

"Fantastic," said Glenn. "I am looking forward to it already and don't think I will sleep with excitement between then and now."

"Is that right, Glenn? OK goodbye," said Amelia.

"Goodbye," said Glenn and hung up. That was a fantastic call he didn't think ringing a stuffy Professor in the British Museum would have been so much fun. Added some extra spice for his trip down to London. He booked Thursday and Friday off work in the diary and gave Brian a ring.

Unfortunately, Brian couldn't get the days off at this late notice, so Glenn agreed to go down on his own. On Tuesday, he booked the train tickets for eight am Thursday morning out of Manchester Piccadilly, which would give him enough time to walk to the museum according to the map of London he had picked up earlier. He found a local hotel in Bloomsbury from the phone book and booked in there for one night. He was still keeping a log of the expenses on his little list and was still spending Granddad Victor's pot of money.

Everything was set for Thursday and the next phase of the adventure. They had decided he would just take one coin to London with him rather than lots, just in case something happened down there. If the professor could help, he would then tell him they had a lot more.

Chapter 40

Glenn was up early at six am. He had packed his case the night before so took a quick shower and got ready. He decided to keep the coin on him. There was no way he was going to let it off his person during the whole trip. He looked at the wardrobe where another three hundred and fifty coins lay ready to hopefully set out their future. There was one missing because Brian had decided he wanted to carry a coin around with him as a lucky charm. Glenn warned him though, "Don't go flashing it around yet." They didn't want to attract any additional attention before a plan was in place. To date that practice of keeping a low profile since returning from Egypt had paid off.

He was getting a lift into Manchester from Dad. He worked just next to Manchester Piccadilly and, although he didn't start work until eight am, he always left the house at seven regularly as clockwork to beat the traffic. Normally a pain in the neck this habit, today it served Glenn perfectly. He locked up and set off on the walk to his parent's house. Another unusual trait of Dad's was he would gladly offer you a lift, but you had to be at the car at the right time else he would just simply leave you and he wouldn't go out of his journey's way to pick anyone up. No one was allowed to disturb Dad's routine.

The journey to Piccadilly went to plan and Glenn arrived on the concourse. He had never taken a train to London and this was another first in his adventures over the last six months. He thought he had never killed anyone before, but could tick that one off now as well. He suddenly felt gloomy at that and had to snap himself out of it. He asked a guard for directions to the right train and platform rather than trying to work out the display boards himself. He took his seat, stashed his overnight bag in the rack above and settled back for the journey. He found himself feeling very excited. The train set off spot on time and away he went.

After ninety minutes, he took out his map of London. According to the map, the walk from Euston to Bloomsbury and the British Museum looked straightforward enough. It didn't even look like a mile, a fifteen-minute walk at the most so he should be there in plenty of time for his meeting at noon. He hated being late for anything so always planned to get there early and, therefore, had some time up his sleeve if something went wrong. He had decided to use the spare time to have a look around the Egyptian exhibition at the museum, perhaps just to get a feel for ancient Egypt and if the coins felt like they belonged.

He got to the museum and chatted to the receptionist to ask where the Egyptian exhibition was. She smiled and announced proudly that they had seven permanent Egyptian galleries! He followed her directions and made his way to the Egyptian exhibition.

He found himself absolutely amazed by what was on show. Maybe it was because he had been there, but he really felt a bond with the treasures. There must have been over a hundred mummies and coffins, knives, weapons, ivory statues, Granite statues absolutely everything. It struck him how the ancient Egyptians seemed obsessed with death and the afterlife. Were his coins the result of a robbery a hundred years ago. The stash of some rich Egyptian god that he had buried with him for his afterlife.

He came across a bronze statue of a cat. It stood about forty centimetres high and it was remarkably beautiful. The inscription said it was believed to be almost as old as 664 BC. How did they make such items almost three thousand years ago? Incredible. What he hadn't seen though were any coins. He could have easily missed them but was that good news if they didn't have any and he did. Then he had a feeling of doom and gloom. Maybe they didn't have any because ancient Egyptian coins didn't exist, and they had something else. Something that wasn't worth anything!

He looked at his watch and noticed it was already nearly noon. Where had that time gone? He walked back to the reception desk and explained he had a meeting with Professor Montgomery at midday. She gave him directions and he set off with a great purpose for the most important meeting of his life. And don't forget to throw the lovely Amelia into the mix as well. He found he had a spring in his step.

Chapter 41

He found the office with the name plate on the door:

Professor Montgomery
Senior Curator, Ancient Egypt; Papyri

This must be the place. He didn't know what Papyri was, but he hoped it had something to do with coins. The door was ajar, so he knocked and went it. It was exactly like the office he was expecting. The room was deserted although he could hear voices coming from somewhere. Bookcases lined the walls, full of books all around the room. Something you would expect Indiana Jones's office to look like. There was a desk to one side with a name plate on it that simply said:

Amelia Fountain-Holmes

Wow! That was some name god only knows what she would make of Glenn when they finally met. A door opened to the right and Glenn's heart literally skipped a beat. In came a real-life goddess after all the dead ones he had been looking at in the museum. She was wearing a light-grey skirt and white blouse. She had jet-black hair tied back in a ponytail that hung down the centre of her back. She had the most dazzling smile and really deep brown eyes that were framed with the sexiest glasses he had ever seen. As she walked through the door, he noticed her high heels and tanned muscled calves. If she was surprised to see him in her office, she didn't show it.

"Mr Mulligan, I presume," she said holding out here right hand to greet him.

"Amelia Fountain-Holmes, I presume," said Glenn, taking her hand and shaking it a little too eagerly. "That is some name," he said. "You don't get many names like that around our way."

"Is that so, Mr Mulligan," she replied.

"Yes, and please call me Glenn," he said. He was so stunned by how she looked that he immediately said to himself back off, *You have absolutely no chance, mate. Get a good price for the coins and leg it without making a complete fool of yourself.*

"Ah, Glenn, yes I remember our first conversation. Did you have a good trip down to the smoke as we called it?"

"Yes, it's been a great day so far. I arrived early so I spent an hour or so looking around your Egyptian galleries, but I need loads more time to study them in detail. I thought it was absolutely fascinating."

"We are really proud of our exhibits, especially the Egyptian ones, but we are a bit biased in this office as you can imagine. As I said on the phone, we have the biggest collection of Egyptian antiquities in the world outside Egypt itself. Do you know we have over one hundred thousand pieces on site? Not all on display at once of course, most of them are down in the archives. I could give you a tour if you like?"

"I would like that very much. Suddenly I find myself becoming the biggest fan of the British Museum," he said, with a really cheeky smile on his face.

"Quite," she said. "Would you like a cup of coffee? Professor Montgomery will be delayed a few minutes, so he asked me to look after you."

"If the professor wants you to look after me, then who am I to disappoint him," said Glenn.

Amelia picked her pass card up from the desk and led the way out of the office and down the corridor to the kitchen. She used her card to open the door and held it open for Glenn to enter.

"Wow, it must be good coffee if you have to have a security card to get in."

"You have to have your card to get in any room in the museum, Glenn. I'm not promising you the best coffee you have ever had, but it's not too bad. What do you fancy?"

Glenn nearly came back with a cheesy line but thought better of it. "Just white, no sugar please," he said.

Amelia flicked the kettle on and took a couple of cups from the overhead cupboard. "So, this must be exciting, inheriting priceless ancient gold coins."

"It is. Well, it will be if your professor confirms they are ancient that is. My Granddad left them to me, what he called his 'Spoils of War'."

"War spoils, how come?"

"He liberated them from a group of Germans in Egypt in the Second World War."

"Really? Well, thank goodness he did as we would have lost them forever," she said.

"I know it's an incredible story I would love to talk you through it sometime."

"I would like that. Did you get your hotel sorted for tonight or are you planning to head straight back up north?" she said, trying to mock Glenn's northern accent.

"Yes, I am staying in a hotel nearby and I am really glad I decided too as well; as I said earlier, I am going to spend a few more hours looking around the museum while I'm here."

"Excellent news, do you still want a tour guide to show you around?"

"The museum? Yes Please."

Amelia started laughing. "Yes, the museum. I would be happy to show you around and then perhaps you can repay the favour by taking me to dinner tonight?"

"Absolutely. It would be my pleasure," said Glenn.

"OK, that's tonight sorted then. Here's your coffee. Let's go and see if the professor is ready to see you now." She opened the door and led the way back to the office and to the door to the right where she has emerged from ten minutes earlier. She popped her head around the corner "Are you free, sir?" she said.

"Ah yes, Mr Mulligan, Amelia yes please show him in," said the professor.

She came back into the office and said to Glenn, "He's free now you can go in. Good luck." She touched the top of his arm that made the hairs on the back of his neck stand on end. He took a big breath and walked in.

Chapter 42

The professor stood up to meet Glenn and shake his hand, shutting the door behind him and beckoning his to take a seat. "Good afternoon, Mr Mulligan, sorry for the delay. Before we start, I need to point out to you that the museum, and myself as head of department, don't normally do private viewings and assessments of Egyptian artefacts. It's a museum policy. However, you mentioned to Amelia on the phone that you believe you have some rare Egyptian coins and they are a particular passion of mind. Have been my whole life, so I just couldn't resist. I have talked to my superiors and they have given me special permission to continue with this session, so I hope you appreciate the circumstances of this meeting. Now having said all that, how can I be of service to you?"

The professor looked exactly how Glenn thought he would. In fact, he could have described him before he came in. He had hair everywhere! A big beard and loads of grey and brown hair which made it difficult to guess his age. *Probably in his fifties,* thought Glenn. He even had the classic corduroy trousers and elbow-patched old jacket. He looked like everyone's friendly old Granfather.

"So, Mr Mulligan how can I help you?" he beckoned again, following the silence from Glenn.

"I have inherited some coins from my Granddad that he acquired during the war. I was hoping you could tell me what they were and whether they would be valuable and perhaps if the museum might like to buy them from me," said Glenn.

"Well let's not get carried away yet, Mr Mulligan. Can I see them?"

Glenn took the gold coin out of his pocket and handed it over to the professor. The Professor studied it carefully and muttered some words Glenn couldn't understand. He looked up at Glenn. "Yes. this is from Persia. You have here, Mr Mulligan, a coin from the Achaemenid Empire which dates back to something like 485 to 420 BC."

"BC," exclaimed Glenn. "Then that makes it two and a half thousand years old."

"That's right, Mr Mulligan, this is indeed a nice piece. As I said, it's from Persia and the Achaemenid Empire and I am certain this is a coin of Darios the First. You can see here on one side this is a depiction of the Persian king or hero, wearing kidaris and kandys, there's a quiver over the shoulder, in a kneeling or running stance and looks like he is holding a spear."

"Is it rare then or more to the point, is it valuable?"

"Well, I have seen a few of these before but yes as coins go, it's pretty rare. I would say you might get fifteen hundred to two thousand dollars for it. We would certainly like to make you an offer to have it here in the museum."

"That's great news, sir. I knew it had to be old just looking at it."

"You mentioned having some other coins, have you brought them with you?"

"I didn't have to professor, they are all the same kind of coins."

"Ah right that's even better. A collection of these coins might well get you more money for them, but I can't promise anything. I would have to go to my superiors on that. How many have you got?"

"We have three hundred and fifty-two of them, Professor."

"THREE HUNDRED AND FIFTY-TWO," shouted the professor as he looked amazed at Glenn. He sat back down in his chair and let out a big sigh. "How on earth did your Granddad come across that lot? It's a treasure trove all right."

"It's a very long story but while he was based in Egypt, he basically intercepted a group of Germans who were stealing it away and liberated it from them."

"Well, thank goodness he did as it might have been lost forever. We haven't, or rather no one has ever seen a collection as big as that. I don't think the academia world would believe such an amount of coins existed. Are you looking to sell them all?"

"Yes, well most of it anyway. I am splitting it with my brother as we were both left them in my Granddad's will." Glenn thought it was best at this point not to mention that they had gone to Egypt and brought the coins back themselves.

"OK, Mr Mulligan, can you come back tomorrow? I am going to have to ask around a lot of contacts and the museum board to see who would be willing to buy such a huge amount of coins. I hope you have them in a safe place?"

"Yes, I have them locked away in a safe," Glenn lied as he suddenly had a dreaded flashback to the bag in the bottom of the wardrobe. He was thinking two thousand dollars times three hundred and fifty-two coins made a lot of money. A fortune! Oh my god wait until he rings Brian tonight. "Can I just ask, Professor, how many dollars there would be to the pound at the moment?"

"Trying to work out your windfall eh. Well, let me see," he said while he took out a pen and paper and started jotting down numbers. "I think the exchange rate is about 1.7 dollars to the pound. So, if you say two thousand dollars for three hundred and fifty-two coins, comes in at around seven hundred and four thousand dollars or in pounds that would be four hundred and fourteen thousand pounds, give or take a few pounds."

It was Glenn's turn to stand there with his mouth open looking bemused. "That's about thirty years pay!"

"Not a bad inheritance, Mr Mulligan, I would say. Are you happy to leave the coin with me? I will give you a receipt." He wrote one out and handed it to Glenn. "Do you want to make an appointment with Amelia for tomorrow? I am sure she will look after you?"

"She was going to show me around the archives."

"Excellent idea. Tell her to take the afternoon off. She is most definitely at your disposal, Mr Mulligan. Now let me get on to make a few phone calls. Goodbye, Mr Mulligan, and see you tomorrow," he said, shaking Glenn's hand.

Glenn wandered out of the office looking at the receipt in his hand. The professor shut the door behind him.

Chapter 43

Amelia looked up as Glenn came back into the office. He stood there with a bemused look on his face staring at the receipt in his hand. "Everything OK, Glenn?" asked Amelia. "I heard the professor shouting out a bit. I hope he didn't give you a hard time."

"Far from it, Amelia. The coin is old. Two and a half thousand years old to be precise and the professor thinks it could be worth as much as two thousand dollars."

"Wow, that's great Glenn. Does that mean I can have a dessert with my meal tonight?"

"No, you don't understand, Amelia, that's not what the professor was shouting about. He was shouting at the fact that I have over three hundred and fifty of them."

"You're kidding. That's amazing. Congratulations. It's a fortune. You are rich, Glenn."

"I know. I need to sit down and take it in." He still had his coffee cup in his other hand so finished it off. "I need to come back to see the professor tomorrow afternoon and he asked me to ask you to book me an appointment. I think I had better stay over another night, hopefully the hotel will be able to fit me in."

"How does someone in the nineties find a huge treasure chest from two and a half thousand years ago in Egypt?"

"As I said before, that is a very long story, Amelia, and I am more than happy to walk you through it tonight."

"Here's the phone book, give the hotel a call while I have a look in the professor's diary," she said.

He found the number for the hotel and gave them a call. It wasn't a problem and they booked him in for a second night. He only had one spare pair of underpants, but he would get away with that. If he found some time, he would do a bit of shopping.

"OK, that's you booked in at three pm with the professor tomorrow afternoon. How exciting!"

Glenn was beaming now and couldn't stop. "The good news doesn't end there. He also said you can have the afternoon off to show me around the archives."

"Really? Well, it just shows what a pile of gold coins will do to someone's mood."

"To be honest, Amelia, I could really use a drink. Do you fancy blowing off the trip around the archives and duck out to the pub for a few drinks?"

"Now that sounds like a plan, let's go. We can go across to the museum tavern and then do the archive trip afterwards."

They made their way out of the museum and across to the tavern. On the way, Amelia reminded Glenn that she wanted to hear the story about how his Granddad came across the coins and how Glenn and his brother got hold of them. His mind was racing. How much of the story could he tell? He was conscious of the two dead people that would have been found at Mount Himeimat so there was no way he could mention that place. If it did ever come out, then it was just too much of a coincidence to be ignored. He and Brian had decided to take Mount Himeimat out of Victor's written story, but they had never had the conversation as to how and where they got the coins themselves.

While they walked and made small talk, he was running over the story in his head. He could tell her everything of the war stories he had read and just not mention Mount Himeimat. He had to be honest to everyone that he and Brian had gone to Egypt, so he had to stick with that story. He decided to say they left it buried somewhere in El Alamein and hopefully pass over that quickly, so she didn't ask too many questions. In fact, so that no one would ask too many questions.

They entered the bar and took a table. He went to the bar and ordered a pint of London Pride and a glass of white wine. When he returned to the table, he sat down and started to tell his story. He started in Dublin, in 1941.

Amelia seemed wrapped up in the story. She asked loads of questions and asked about the map and how they followed it to recover the treasure, but she didn't seem to come across as suspicious and lapped up the whole story. Glenn was really getting into his part of storyteller and relished the questions and talked about the story and the characters in it he had come to know and love.

About an hour and two drinks later, he came to the part where he had spoken to Amelia for the first time on the phone. "And of course, you know the rest of the developments from there," he said.

"What a brilliant story and what an interesting man Granddad Victor sounds. I wish I would have met him; you don't get to see many characters like that anymore," she said.

"Hahaha," Glenn laughed at that. "I am not sure what you would have made of the 1990s Victor compared to the dashing stories of the war, but you are right, he was a real character and also in my eyes, a real hero. Not to mention his buddies. They were all heroes."

"Glenn, let me be the first person to buy you a drink after your good news."

"That would be really nice," he said.

In fact, they had two more before noticing the clock was moving towards four pm. "No time now to have a look around the archives, perhaps you could come in early tomorrow and we can do it then?"

"Sure, that sounds great. Now what's the plan tonight?"

"Well, I need to go home and get changed out of these work clothes."

Glenn was thinking, *Hardly work clothes, you look fantastic in them.*

"If it's your first night out in London, then we should go into Covent Garden. You will love the atmosphere. There's a nice restaurant where we can meet. Shall we say seven pm?" she said, writing down the name of the restaurant on a piece of paper produced from her bag.

"OK, it's a date," he said tucking the paper into his pocket and standing up. He ushered Amelia out through the door and stood on the street. He felt a bit awkward, what should he do now? She made his mind up by saying goodbye and heading off into the crowds.

He almost skipped down the street in the direction of the hotel. He couldn't wait for tonight and he also couldn't wait for his conversation with Brian!

Chapter 44

He jumped out of the shower and collapsed on the bed trying to remember everything the professor had said. It was ten to six and he had arranged with Brian to give him a ring at six. He got up, a squirt of Lynx and some aftershave and threw on the only pair of jeans and shirt he had brought down with him. If he was lucky enough to get a second night out tomorrow with Amelia, he was going to have to try and buy another shirt.

He had decided to use the phone in the hotel room rather than speaking about the gold coins in the lobby or in a phone box on a street corner. The only drawback was a ten-minute call was going to cost three or four pounds but hey, he had four hundred thousand to play with, didn't he! He picked up the receiver and dialled the number. Mum answered and shouted for Brian.

"Hey there," he said. "How's life down there in London then?"

"Hi Brian, couldn't be any better, mate, it all went really well."

"Go on."

"The professor says the coin is genuine. It's from some empire two and a half thousand years ago."

"Jesus, that's amazing, Glenn. How much is it all worth then?"

"About two thousand dollars, the professor said, which is about one thousand, seven hundred pounds."

"OK, I suppose although I was hoping for a lot more. Don't forget, Glenn, what we went through to get those bloody coins. I mean, I won't turn my nose up at the money but was hoping for a windfall, that's all."

"What the hell are you on about, man? I mean two thousand dollars for one coin not the whole bloody lot of them."

"Wooahh, that's more like it, mate. How much is that then?"

"The professor is saying just over four hundred grand for the lot." Brian whistled down the phone at this sum of money. "Now we haven't sold them yet though, so we need to be a bit cautious and not get carried away until we have a deal in the bag. The professor is speaking to the museum and to some private collectors in America that he knows. He thinks the private collectors would offer more but he would love the coins to go into the museum and I am inclined to agree with him."

"Well, whatever you think, Glenn, if you can bring that sort of money home with you, it would all have been well worth it."

"I am booked in to see him tomorrow at three, so I am going to stay down here another night, so I have plenty of time to get the deal done. But I am worried now about those coins sitting there in the bottom of my wardrobe in an empty house."

"I was just thinking the same thing, mate. I will go around and stay at yours until you get back. So, you're staying another night then? That sounds sensible what are you going to do tonight then?"

"Well, funny you should mention that; I have a date with that sexy sounding secretary, Amelia. She is absolutely stunning and even better looking than I could have possibly imagined from the phone conversation."

"Haha, well you just behave yourself and don't go telling her all our secrets. Remember you are down there for the coins and nothing else."

"I'm not that daft. I told her the story but never mentioned the mount and said Victor buried it in El Alamein. She seemed to believe that so that has to be our story from now on."

"OK, you don't have to tell me; I am getting used to keeping secrets. I won't tell anyone anything until that money is in the bank. Have a good night and give me a call tomorrow at the same time."

"Will do, mate, see you later."

With that, Glenn put the phone down and picked up his jacket. He got out the map of London and picked out a route to walk to Covent Garden. It was a nice night so he would enjoy the half hour walk. Six fifteen time to go.

Walking across London was a strange experience to a northern lad. The place and pavements were packed never mind the roads that were absolutely grid locked and you never heard an English spoken voice. It was so cosmopolitan, and Glenn thought, *This isn't the capital of England, it's the capital of the world!* But he hadn't seen anything yet until he arrived in Covent Garden. Oh yes what a place this was. It was alive with excitement and he loved it straight away. This was the place to be. He wandered around for ten minutes until he found the restaurant. He took a deep breath and gathered himself before entering.

Amelia was already there he was pleased to see but she looked different. She had her hair down and no glasses, tight fitting jeans and a rather tired-looking baggy jumper which he guessed had to be trendy. This was the second time he had seen her for the first time today and for the second time she took his breath away. She smiled when she saw him approaching the table and stood up and greeted him with a kiss on the cheek. *Well, that's a full house*, thought Glenn, *she even smells delicious.*

He sat down and they ordered drinks and food. They chatted the night away about themselves and about the coins. Amelia wanted to hear the story of Victor again, so Glenn ran through it with his audience seeming to like it even more the second time. The time flew by and it was nearly ten o'clock before they realised.

"We had better vacate the table. I think they are starting to wonder if we are ever going to leave," said Amelia.

"I will get the bill and meet you out front," said Glenn.

"All sorted?" she said as he exited the restaurant.

"Yep, all sorted. Now can I walk you home?"

"Well, I live with my parents over by Holland Park, it would take us over an hour to walk it."

"Oh right, I have absolutely no idea where Holland Park is. How do you normally get home then?"

"I usually just grab a tube from Holborn. Let's walk that way and perhaps stop off at a pub for a last one and then you can see me onto the tube."

"Sure, but is that safe? I would rather walk you home."

"Haha, don't be silly I do the tube twice a day; it's absolutely fine."

"OK, let's go and find that pub then."

The strolled off and found a pub for one last drink. Glenn couldn't believe how disappointed he felt when they left the pub and headed for the tube station. The tube station was on the other side of the road and Amelia took his hand while they dashed across. When they got to the other side, she said, "Oh no, I think I have something in my eye."

"Let me have a look," said Glenn. She stood there looking up at him and he was looking into her eyes. He was lost in them.

"Can you see anything?"

"No, sorry can't see a thing; it looks OK to me," he said.

She sighed an almost sounded disappointed before finally pulling away. She turned to the tube entrance and looked back. "Goodnight, Glenn Mulligan, thank you for a lovely evening."

"Goodnight, Amelia," and with that she was gone.

Glenn was kicking himself. *She wanted you to kiss her you idiot and you absolutely blew it,* he thought. *You bloody stupid idiot, I can't believe you bottled it. What on earth must she think?* He stood there for a few minutes, hoping she might come back out, but she didn't. He eventually, reluctantly turned away and started the walk back to his hotel. In a terrific mood but reprimanding himself all the way home for being such a wimp!

Chapter 45

He woke just after nine am and got dressed and made his way down to the breakfast room. This was going to be some day, so he decided to have the full English breakfast with extra sausage and egg. After breakfast, he was going to go into the museum early to see if Amelia had time to show him around the archives. He was genuinely interested in them but of course he also wanted to spend some more time with her. He also wanted to see if she was still interested after he sloped off with such a whimper last night.

He arrived at the museum just before twelve and although he thought he knew his way to Amelia's office, he checked in at reception for guidance. The receptionist confirmed what he thought was the route, with a little correction, and he set off to what felt like his day of destiny. When he arrived and went into the office, he was unbelievably disappointed not to find Amelia there. What should he do take a seat and wait? What if she had gone for an early lunch, he could be sat there for an hour. He decided to have a look at the books in the bookcase.

One of his favourite things to do was to spend time looking through the books in the various bookshops whenever he went shopping. Books fascinated him and he could always lose himself looking through the authors, trying to pick out books he had read and looking for sequels that might take his fancy. Mind you, he wasn't likely to find any Ken Follet, Wilbur Smith or Tom Clancy on these shelves.

He picked up a book on Egyptian artefacts and was flicking through it when he heard a voice behind him. "My, Mr Mulligan, you are extremely early; we are not due to meet until three, are we?" He turned around to see the friendly face of the professor.

"No, sir," he said. "I was hoping to catch Amelia and see if I could get that trip around the archives first."

"Right you are, she has just popped off to run an errand for me, should be back any minute. I have nearly got all the details for our meeting; I am just waiting for a call from the States and hopefully, I will have some good news to share with you later."

"That is good news, sir."

"Carry on, Mr Mulligan, see you later," and the professor and went back into his office, shutting the door behind him.

Glenn went back to reading the book on Egyptian Artefacts and sat in Amelia's chair while he did. "Well, well,

Mr Mulligan, are you after my job?" came a familiar voice as he looked up from his book.

"Good morning, Amelia, how are you? I was just catching up on some artefacts, now of course I am an expert," he said, grinning.

"It's afternoon already, Glenn, but I am absolutely fine. And how's our artefact dealer this morning. Hangover by any chance?"

"No, actually I am OK although I had a lie in and a huge breakfast to make sure. What about you did you get home OK?"

"Yes, all went fine. Thanks for a nice night out, I really enjoyed it."

"Great. Same again tonight?"

"I normally wash my hair on a Friday, but I will make an exception for you."

"Thank the lord for that," he said, laughing. "I was hoping you might be able to show me around the archives, but it looks like you are busy."

"We are waiting for an important call from the States, concerning your coins actually; once that comes in and the professor is happy, I should have some time."

"OK, I will get out of your hair then and go back to the Egyptian galleries. If you get chance to break away, you will find me there; if not, I will be back before three for the professor."

He had probably spent about 30 minutes in the gallery when Amelia found him looking at the cat again. She reported all was well, the professor had taken the call he was expecting, and she had a couple of hours to show him around.

They spent the whole two hours wandering around the archives, looking at all sorts of relics with Amelia talking Glenn through the various pieces and how they came to be in the museum. He was really impressed by her knowledge but as she said she had been living this job for the last four years since leaving college. It suddenly occurred to Glenn that he didn't know how old she was. Four years since college should make here 22 or 23. The older women then! He would ask her later.

In plenty of time for the meeting with the professor, they made their way back to her office. They waited there patiently for three pm. Glenn kept looking at his watch until finally the professor popped his head out of the door. "Ready for you now, Mr Mulligan," he announced.

Chapter 46

Glenn jumped up and followed him to his office, seeing a reassuring whispered good luck from Amelia on his way. He sat down in the chair opposite the professor's desk and waited for his fate. The professor organised a few pieces of paper on his desk, with his notepad and pen and looked up at Glenn.

"Hopefully, I have some good news for you. A find this size has caused a considerable amount of interest in the market as you can imagine. There are many experts jumping up and down all over the world eager to see this hoard and find out all about it. That's good for you as high demand always helps to push the price up."

"That does sound like good news," said Glenn who found he was gripping the sides of the chair firmly like he did when he was at the dentist.

"OK, I have a few options for you. You mentioned three hundred and fifty-two coins but that you, and your brother, would like to keep a coin for yourselves and, therefore, I have made it known to my peers there are three hundred and fifty coins in the collection up for sale. I have to say, Mr Mulligan, that I am a bit selfish here and I would like the coins, or some of them, to be displayed at the museum."

"I spoke to my brother last night, Professor, and he agreed that we would also like to do that if at all possible."

"That's very reassuring but at least wait to hear what I have to say first. Now my private contact in the States, the call I was waiting for before, is very interested in buying the coins. He believes each coin would be worth in the region of one thousand seven hundred dollars each. But he would like to buy the entire collection and, therefore, would pay up to six hundred and twenty-five thousand dollars. And before you get you calculator out, I have worked that out at three hundred and sixty-seven thousand pounds."

"Wow, that is incredible. Obviously not as much as we thought yesterday but still a fortune."

"There are two other options I would like you to consider, Mr Mulligan. First, I have been to the board of the museum and we too would like to buy the whole collection. Unfortunately, though we can't afford to match the offer from the States. The most the museum can go to is three hundred and thirty thousand pounds. I understand, Mr Mulligan, it's less than the other offer, but we hope you will consider it favourably."

"That is still very generous, Professor, and, of course, we will look on your offer favourably. It would be great to keep the coins in England and in the museum. You mentioned another option?"

"There is. It's a split of the coins with the museum buying ten coins for twenty thousand pounds. To display here. The only issue with this is, it's not a favourite of our American buyer as his collection then would not be unique. He will still buy the remaining three hundred and forty coins but at a much more reduced rate of two hundred and eighty thousand pounds."

"Hmm that doesn't sound as good as the first two options," said Glenn. "I think I will put the two first options to my brother for consideration and come back to you with our answer."

"That's great, Mr Mulligan. Without wishing you to be persuaded too much, if you chose the museum, we could come and collect the coins next week and have the money in your account by the weekend."

"That's fantastic. My brother will be at work at the moment, but I could try and give him a call."

"Here's my phone and I will step outside to give you some privacy." The professor stood up, offering Glenn his chair before leaving the office and closing the door behind him.

Glenn dialled the number and Brian answered, "Hi, Brian, it's me."

"An early call, mate, that's either really good news or bad news. Go on hit me with it," said Brian.

"It's definitely good news. I am in the professor's office now. He has just stepped out to give us a few minutes to chat it through. He has got us two deals to consider. Brace yourself mate. Three hundred and sixty-seven thousand pounds from the American buyer and Three hundred and thirty thousand from the museum here. He did add that if we picked the museum, he could have the money in our bank accounts by next weekend. What do you think?"

"I just can't believe this. It's so much money, Glenn. Obviously, we should go for the American, shouldn't we? Thirty-seven grand more has to be worth considering."

"True, but I don't know anything about selling things to America. Would it mean we have to go over there and then get into a bargaining thing? If you're asking my opinion, mate, I would go with the museum. We have the deal nailed by next weekend and we would be rich. One hundred and sixty-five grand each. It would take me about thirteen years to earn that amount."

"Are you sure? It would be an end to all this, and it would be great to get the money in the bank and stop all this worrying and wondering. OK, I am happy to go with your gut feel, Glenn, let's go with the museum."

"OK, let's do it. I will go and shake on it with the professor and give you a call at six to let you know if everything is sorted."

"Speak to you later, Glenn. And, Glenn, you did a really good job there, mate, well done."

"Cheers, Brian."

Glenn put the phone down and let out a big sigh of relief. He stood up and crossed to the office door and opened it into Amelia's office. The professor and Amelia were both stood looking anxious. They looked at Glenn. "We would love to accept the offer from the museum," said Glenn.

The two of them literally jumped for joy and the professor shook Glenn's hand vigorously while Amelia threw her arms around him.

"Terrific news, Mr Mulligan. I will get a contract of sale drawn up for us to sign and we can arrange the details of transfer next week," said the professor.

"Thank you, sir. Would it be OK for me to whisk Miss Fountain-Holmes off for a celebratory drink?"

"Absolutely. If you call in tomorrow before you get the train home, I will have the paperwork ready for you to sign."

Chapter 47

Glenn's London education provided by Amelia was to have another night. They had decided not to go straight to the pub this time but to go and freshen up and meet in Leicester Square at six. Glenn was pleased about this decision as he had run out of clothes and didn't fancy going out again with Amelia in the same shirt and jeans he went out in last night. He still had a sizeable cash kitty he had brought with him and wanted to get some new clothes to feel good for the night ahead. He had noticed a River Island shop in the morning, so he headed off there and treated himself to a whole new outfit including a new rather dashing pair of shoes.

He set off for Leicester Square, finding a phone box on the way. He reported in with Brian and said he was going to sign the paperwork in the morning and make the arrangements with the professor about handing over the coins to the museum sometime next week. Brian was happy and was also getting ready to go out and celebrate. He was slightly amused to hear Glenn was going on another date with Amelia and told him not to do anything stupid which would involve buying a ring. Glenn told him to bugger off. Before he hung up, he agreed to call in and see Brian as soon as he got home tomorrow so he could read through the agreement himself. They also decided to go out together and celebrate on the Saturday night. But that was tomorrow, and tonight was about Amelia.

It seemed impossible that anywhere could be busier than Covent Garden, but Leicester Square was alive. It was absolutely buzzing, and Glenn drank in the atmosphere while he waited for Amelia. There were pubs, shops and the big cinemas that he had seen on TV where the big red-carpet nights happened. There were also street artists of all kinds. A juggler juggling fire torches, there were three bands in total and lots of pop up stalls selling souvenirs. Again, every accent imaginable could be heard as people wandered around taking in the entertainment. Glenn was so engrossed, he never even noticed Amelia approach him.

"Enjoying yourself, are you?" she said.

"What a place. It's just so much fun. Thanks for suggesting this, Amelia," he replied as he kissed her on the cheek. He decided after his feeble ending last night, was it only last night, it seemed weeks ago; he was going to take every opportunity to hold her hand, get close and kiss her as often as he could. For all he knew, he was going home tomorrow, and this might be the last chance he would get to take her out. And if it was, he was going to have no regrets.

"You look nice tonight," she said, standing back and admiring his new look.

"Thanks. I thought I had better smarten myself up, I only brought one shirt down with me," he said, grinning sheepishly.

"I like it it's very nice."

"So, what's the plan tonight?"

"I thought we could do a few bars around here, grab something to eat and then we could walk down to Trafalgar Square and Westminster which are impressive in the evening. We could finish with a few drinks on the Southbank before grabbing the last tube around twelve."

"Wow, you have it all planned out, don't you? Sounds good to me. Come on, that looks a nice place, the first drink is on me."

"I hope more than the first drink is on you after your windfall. Don't forget I am merely a humble secretary," she said, teasing him.

"Yes, who lives in Hollands Way or road or whatever nice district of London it is. Which is a million miles away from the north and Oldham."

"Hollands Park, Glenn, and don't remind me where you live as you will be going back tomorrow and that is a long way away."

"But I will be back next week, and we still have tonight."

"We sure do."

He took her hand and she seemed happy to give it. They walked into the nearest bar and put Amelia's plan into action. They talked all night, sometimes about the coins and the inheritance and Glenn's trip to Egypt but not all night. They talked more about themselves and the lives they were leading. As they did it became even more apparent to Glenn just how different their lives were.

Amelia had grown up in quite a lavish, comfortable and happy home. She had graduated from university and the role at the museum was her first job in the real world. She specialised in Egyptology which had always fascinated her growing up. The job with the professor was her dream job and she hoped to learn as much as she could from him, and all the facilities offered by the museum. She talked about how she would build a career in this field and hoped to go on expeditions of her own to Egypt and around the world. To become a recognised expert like the professor was her ultimate goal. Glenn was so impressed with her commitment to this vision.

Glenn felt second best when he talked about himself. He hadn't gone to university and had left school at the earliest opportunity and joined a big corporate. He could see a career in this industry and there were lots of scope for promotion and increased responsibility, and he guessed that's where he would go, but he had no clear vision or self-determination to make this happen like Amelia did. Talking to her made Glenn think about his own life.

If she was disappointed with his career dynamic, she didn't show it and seemed really interested with his stories of the HR world and the people he worked with. Maybe working in a museum was not always as exciting as it sounded and some of the stories Glenn told on wild Christmas parties and the like made his office sound like a fun place to work.

They made their way down to Trafalgar Square where he got the opportunity to splash her in a playful way. He regretted not having a camera yet again to capture some of these memories. They walked across Westminster Bridge and looked back to the houses of parliament which were all floodlit and looked very impressive. While they stood in this magical place, he took the opportunity to kiss her properly for the first time. It was everything and more he had hoped for. The build-up over these two days and the close proximity they had to each other had added to their passion and as they broke away and continued walking it felt like they had been a couple for ages. When in fact, they only met yesterday morning!

Glenn walked her to the tube station, but this time said goodnight properly before watching her walk away into the tube. Like last night, he stood outside just in case she came back out but of course she didn't, so he took out his London map to see where he was and plan out a route back to the hotel.

He noticed he was about two miles away in Waterloo. As they had enjoyed the evening, they had slowly moved further and further away. Although it was late, there were loads of people around and Glenn was going to enjoy the walk back. He was on top of the world. Life was good!

They had arranged to meet for breakfast the following morning and then walk to the museum together. The professor was already there before them and ushered Glenn straight into his office. He presented Glenn with a ten-page document and talked him through the important bits. He did say it may well be worth him getting his solicitor to have a look through it for his own piece of mind before he signed it. Glenn thought, *I don't have a solicitor.* But he didn't tell the professor that and said he would get him to look at it this week. Once he had the go ahead from his solicitor, the professor required him to sign the document and fax it back down to him, Amelia would give him the number, as soon as he could next week to get the process in motion.

The main parts of the contract stated that the museum would pay the sum of three hundred and thirty thousand pounds into Glenn's account once the coins had been authenticated by the professor and one other expert, provided by the museum, which they would do next Friday when Glenn would bring them back down. They put a twelve-noon meeting in the diary and Glenn was already planning a night over and another night out with Amelia before they shook hands on the deal.

Glenn left the office with the paperwork and accepted Amelia's offer to walk him to Euston for his train. The goodbye in Euston Terminal took a long time! They attracted the attention of a lot of passengers, but they didn't care. Eventually Glenn dragged himself away, promising to ring every night before they saw each other again the following Friday. As he boarded the train, he had a huge smile on his face and thought to himself, *That was one very successful trip to London.*

Chapter 48

Brian had read through the paperwork and like Glenn he felt it all sounded straight forward. Almost too good to be true which always got the alarm bells ringing. His dad used to say, "If it's too good to be true, then it isn't!" But both boys couldn't see anything that could go wrong. They arranged to meet a solicitor in their lunch hour on Tuesday. It wasn't cheap as it was short notice, but they had to get the signed copy faxed back to the professor which Glenn could do from the office. They had thought about just signing it but decided on the peace of mind of having an expert read through it.

The solicitor found nothing unusual about the contract but did ask if the boys could prove they owned the coins? He didn't push the point, but it did worry them a bit. It was discovered treasure, so they had no proof it was theirs only the story left by Victor. Their feeling was finders keepers, no one else owned it, did they? So, they signed the contract and faxed it off. Glenn had to book another day off work to go back down to London, thankfully it was after Easter so very few people wanted time off then, but he got the impression he was starting to annoy his boss with all these last minute requests for days off.

By Tuesday lunchtime, everything was set. Glenn would travel down with the coins on Friday and go straight to the museum for the assessment and hopefully closure of the deal. He would have another night out around London and be back home by Saturday teatime all the richer. They planned on having a party at Glenn's to tell the family about their exploits and their good fortune. Beers were on them.

As Glenn arrived home from work, he was thinking about the party and who to invite. Brian would have to get the beers and snacks on the Saturday while Glenn was travelling back. He would ring him later and make the arrangements. The phone rang before he even had time to sit down. He picked it up. "Glenn, is that you?" a familiar voice said.

"Hi, Amelia, how are you, sexy? I was going to ring later but you have beat me to it," he said.

"Listen, Glenn, something has kicked off here, I have phoned to warn you," she replied.

He heard the concern in her voice and suddenly became serious. "What's happened?"

"There's been a detective here from Scotland Yard and the Egyptian ambassador. Voices were raised in the professor's office and I know he has been trying to ring you, so expect a call. He is still in there with the inspector, but the Egyptian ambassador stormed out about an hour ago."

"Oh no, that doesn't sound good." Glenn was starting to panic, and he felt sick to the stomach. Had they found the bodies and linked it back to him? But, how could they? "What do you think it is?"

"I don't know, Glenn, but if I find anything out, I will ring you straight away. Having said that, if you sit tight the professor will definitely ring you tonight."

"OK, thanks Amelia. I can't think what it's about but really appreciate the heads up."

"Good luck, Glenn, give me a call later."

"Will do, speak to you later."

He put the phone down and started pacing around the front room constantly glancing at the phone. He decided to ring Brian and share the pain, he needed his support. He picked the phone up again and dialled, Brian answered. "Brian, something's happened. Amelia has just tipped me off that the police and the Egyptian ambassador have been in a shouting match with the professor. Apparently, he is going to ring me."

"Oh Shit, what do you think that's about? Surely they can't know about what happened over there?"

"I've no idea, mate, but would appreciate you getting your arse over here for when he rings."

"OK, I am on my way."

True to his word, he was there within ten minutes and that resulted in the both of them pacing around the phone speculating on what might have happened. They straightened their story which didn't involve anything to do with Mount Himeimat. Glenn had earlier destroyed the treasure map instructions on where to find the treasure which the boys reckoned could be easily explained. They had then read through Victor's story and took out the pages that referred to the camp and Mount Himeimat. The story still read OK to them. Maybe an expert might pick out the missing pages, but it still read sensibly.

Tensions were so high when the phone rang. Glenn looked at Brian and picked it up. "Hello," he said.

"Hello, Mr Mulligan, it's Professor Montgomery here. Sorry to disturb you but we have a bit of a situation down here."

"Oh right," Glenn said, trying to keep the panic out of his voice. "What's wrong, Professor?"

"Procedures dictated that I had to inform the Egyptian authorities of your find. More out of politeness than anything as nothing of real valuable has appeared on this scale for years, so normally it's just a curtesy call. However, this is a significant find and the Egyptians are not happy at all that you took it from their country without permission. You see some time ago, there were a number of changes to the antiquities laws in Egypt, leading to the suspension of policies allowing finds to be exported out of the country."

"I see, but we didn't know that."

"Exactly, Mr Mulligan, that is what I have explained but unfortunately, that's not the way they see it. They say you deliberately smuggled the treasure out of the country and, therefore, broke the law. I'm afraid they are asking for you to return to Egypt with the treasure to face charges."

"Oh my god, what am I going to do?"

"Don't panic, Mr Mulligan, I am sure we can resolve this. I have Detective Inspector Evans here from Scotland Yard and he has your best interests at heart. But we do need you to come down to London with the coins so we can sort all this out."

"I have booked the day off Friday to travel down, Professor."

"Sorry, Mr Mulligan, but I'm afraid it can't wait. DI Evans will send a car up to pick you up tomorrow morning first thing. I have agreed with him that Amelia can accompany you, so you have a familiar face with you for the journey down. Expect them to arrive about nine am."

"Thank you, Professor."

"My pleasure and please, don't worry too much for now. I am sure this can all be sorted out. DI Evans has booked you into a hotel for your stay, but I will meet you at Scotland Yard when you arrive, and we can take it from there. Good evening,

Mr Mulligan, see you in the morning," said the professor and hung up.

Glenn replaced the receiver very slowly and a very anxious Brian asked, "Well, what they hell was that all about?"

"Nothing about bodies or murder so that's a good sign! Apparently, the Egyptians have accused me of smuggling the treasure out of their country, breaking some antiquity law or something. Scotland Yard have got involved, sounds like they are defending us for now, but they are sending a car up for me in the morning to go back down to London. And they want me to take the coins back down to London with me."

"Bloody hell, they are not hanging around, are they? I am coming with you, of course."

"No. They didn't mention anything about you so let's keep you out of it for now. It might be pretty useful to have you out and about and free; you might need to get the solicitor involved, etc."

"Are you sure? It feels like I am dropping you right in it on your own."

"No. I am not being a martyr or anything but no point both of us facing the music if we don't have too."

"OK, let's keep it positive. Nothing has happened yet, but I thought it was all going to bloody smoothly."

"I know so did I. Come on, let's go down to the pub. I need a few beers after that call; my nerves are absolutely shot.

Mind you, I will have to be back earlyish as I will need to pack for the morning."

"All right, beers are on me, mate," said Brian.

Chapter 49

Glenn was stood by the window looking out into the street the following morning. His bag was packed and his rucksack full of the gold coins and they were waiting by the door. He looked at his watch. Quarter to nine. He'd been told to expect them about nine am depending on the traffic.

When he woke at six thirty, it suddenly dawned on him that Amelia would be seeing his house for the first time. That was enough to get him out of bed and tidy and clean as much as he could. He was very proud of his little town house but of course, it wouldn't compare to a high-status house in Hollands Park as Amelia had described where she lived. Nevertheless, he wanted Amelia to see his place at its best. He had two second-hand sofas and TV, but the carpet was new, and he had decorated throughout himself and installed a new kitchen. He only had a cheap brand of tea and coffee, but it would have to do if they had chance to take one.

He looked out again. Time was really dragging now. His emotions were all over the place. Yes, he was going to see Amelia again and that thought always made his stomach jump, but he was being escorted by Scotland Yard in a police car to London and that doesn't happen to everyone every day. Nothing yet. He made another tour around his house and back to the front window. It didn't take long to do a lap around the house, and he managed a few more.

Eventually, a black BMW car, with the windows blacked out, pulled up. That's a positive, at least it didn't have 'Police' written all over it. Mind you, it would certainly get any neighbours guessing if they saw him leaving in it. A tall good-looking guy got out of the driver's side and Amelia stepped out of the back. She beat him to the path first and headed to the house. She was dressed formally as though she was back at the museum.

Glenn opened the door before she knocked, and she put her arms around his neck and kissed him on the cheek. She pulled away. "Good morning to you," she said. "Are you OK?"

"Well, I didn't sleep too well but me and Brian had a few beers last night so that helped. How was your journey up?"

"It was fine although I have been up since four! I might well have a sleep on your shoulder on the way back."

"Anytime."

She turned around and introduced her travelling partner, "This is Detective Williamson, Glenn."

They shook hands, "Good Morning, Mr Mulligan. I hope we find you well this morning. Sorry for the early start but my boss would like to talk to you this afternoon."

"Good morning, Detective. Am I actually under arrest here?" said Glenn.

"No, nothing like that, Glenn, can I call you Glenn?" Glenn nodded. "I am not fully aware of what's going on, but my instructions are to bring you back down to London with a consignment of three hundred and fifty gold coins. I need to count them and verify that with you. I will then give you a receipt and take them into our custody for now. But I don't have any handcuffs look," he said lifting his jacket up and smiling. "It's all very civilised and my boss told me to tell you there are no charges against you at this time. You are literally helping us with our enquiries."

"OK thanks, Detective, that is really encouraging and put my mind a rest a little."

"Glenn, I could really use a comfort break," said Amelia.

"Sure thing, Amelia, straight at the top of the stairs. Would you both like a tea or coffee?"

"Tea milk and two sugars for me," said the Detective.

"Tea milk, no sugar for me please, Glenn," said Amelia.

"Sweet enough," said Glenn, smiling at her.

"I hope so," she said, disappearing up the stairs.

Glenn picked up the rucksack and passed it to Detective Williamson, "All the coins are in here if you want to start the count while I put the kettle on."

"Thanks," he said and sat down on the carpet, unzipped the rucksack and poured the coins out onto the floor. "Wooah, would you look at that lot."

"I must have done that fifty times and it always takes my breath away," said Glenn as he went off to the kitchen.

He heard Amelia coming back downstairs and heard a cry of "wow" as she too saw the pile of gold coins for the first time. She came into the kitchen. "I've heard you tell the story several times about the coins, but it really is an impressive hoard. I really hope it all works out for you, Glenn," she said as she put her arms around him from behind while he was pouring hot water into three mugs.

He turned around to face her. "So do I, Amelia, this could change my life, our life even." She blushed at that and looked away. He took the milk out of the fridge and topped the brews up discarding the old tea bags in the bin. He took two and left Amelia with her cup and they re-entered the front room. The detective was making progress and had several piles of ten coins stacked up in rows. Glenn put the mugs of tea down and watched the detective. Unsurprisingly, the detective announced three hundred and fifty coins exactly. There had to be as he counted them into the bag in the morning, but he never took it for granted.

It then struck Glenn that the professor had kept to his word by not telling anyone about the coins Glenn and Brian had kept back for themselves. *Good on him,* he thought.

The detective sat on the sofa and started to drink his tea. He took out a receipt pad and jotted down the details. Signing it himself on behalf of Scotland Yard and he handed it to Glenn. "OK, let's finish the tea, quick toilet break and we can head straight off." He stood up, repacked the rucksack and threw it over his shoulder before starting to climb the stairs. He turned around. "I've been told not to let these out of my sight once they were in my possession," he said.

"It's actually reassuring to have a police escort with the coins back to London. Before all this, I was going to have to carry them down myself on the train, so one good thing has come out of this at least," said Glenn.

"Oh, one more thing," said Williamson. "Can you give me your passport? I need to take that back with me as well. Just in case you fancy taking a little holiday?"

They set off back. The coins in the front with Detective Williamson and Amelia in the back with Glenn, holding his hand. As she suspected, she slept for an hour or so on his shoulder. He loved it and stayed very still. He never wanted her to wake up and stay asleep on his shoulder. He felt like a million dollars and she smelled so good.

The journey went without incident and after three hours, they approached London. Glenn had never drove around

London and it amazed him how busy it was. However, compared to Cairo, he would choose London every time. Williamson seemed to know his way around and he took turn after turn, working his way through the back streets until they came to Scotland Yard. He passed through the gates and pulled up and switched off the engine.

"That's us here," he said. "Not a bad journey that, just over three hours and in time for a spot of lunch, I think. Follow me and I will see what the boss wants to do."

They got out of the car. Amelia squeezed Glenn's hand and held onto it as they entered the building. Glenn let out a big sigh and composed himself. What did the rest of this day have instore for him?

They signed in and climbed a set of stairs and entered a room marked 'conference room'. The professor was there waiting for them. He kissed Amelia on the cheek and shook Glenn's hand. "Great to see you both," he said. "Did everything go to plan?"

"I think so," said Glenn.

"I will go and get the boss," said Williamson.

"Just before you do," said the professor. "Is that the gold coins?" he said, pointing to the rucksack.

"It is," said Williamson. "Care to have a quick look." He could see the eager look in the professor's eyes.

He opened the top of the rucksack and the professor peered in. "Oh my word," was all he could manage to say. Williamson zipped it back up and left the room.

The three of them were talking through what had happened when the door opened, and Detective Inspector Evans entered.

Chapter 50

"Good afternoon, everyone, Miss Amelia, Professor and you must be Glenn Mulligan," he said, stretching out his hand to shake Glenn's.

Glenn thought that must be a good sign, he's not come straight in and slapped the handcuffs on. "Good afternoon, Inspector, it's good to meet you," he said.

"OK, let's take a seat," he said, "and I will talk you through what's happening and what we plan on doing this afternoon." They all sat around the conference table.

"So it's nearly one pm now and we have the Egyptian ambassador coming into the station at two. Don't panic, Glenn, this is going to be an informal conversation just to meet him and give him chance to air his views. We can discuss in a minute on what we agree you can say to him. I have agreed that the professor can attend that meeting as a friend and support for yourself, Glenn, and also to represent the interests of the museum. Unfortunately, Miss Amelia you will have to wait outside," he said, looking at Amelia.

"Yes that's fine," she said.

Glenn was feeling OK with this so far. It sounded like the inspector would represent his best interests and he would have the professor in there for support.

"Detective Williamson should be here in a minute with a selection of sandwiches and some tea and coffee. As soon as he gets here, I want to run through your story, Glenn, about how you came in possession of the gold and how you brought it back to the UK. So, you might want to start thinking about how you go about it," he said.

Glenn decided there and then, without any mention of Mount Himeimat, he would stick to the truth as best he could as he agreed with Brian. It felt like his best chance to get out of this in one piece. The door opened and Williamson came in pushing a trolley of food and drink. They all helped themselves to a plate of sandwiches and sat down. The detective inspector encouraged Glenn to take them all through the story while he took notes and they had their lunch. A working lunch he called it.

Glenn started at the beginning and the letter from his Granddad following his unfortunate death. He talked through the highlights of his story. Dublin to Dorset to Egypt and back. The fight with the Germans and the recovery of the gold which they hid outside El Alamein near the coast. He talked about his trip to Egypt and the recovery of the gold. How straight forward it was and how they brought it back in their suitcases. It was at this point, following some questioning from the detective inspector, that Glenn admitted Brian had come to Egypt with him.

He emphasised that he wasn't aware of any laws against bringing treasure out of Egypt and that he believed the gold was stolen by the Germans and eventually came to him. He hadn't anticipated that anyone had owned it.

"Well, that's the first issue I have with the ambassador's claim. He too cannot prove who owned it and he has no records anywhere in Egypt that says whose gold it was or where it came from. That works on your side to some extent, Glenn," he said. "And that's it, Glenn? No more to the story?"

"No that's it," replied Glenn.

"I believe you got the gold back to the UK before Christmas so why did you wait six months to contact the professor?"

"We just didn't know what to do with it. We enjoyed having the gold. It felt brilliant but eventually we thought we needed to try and get some money for it and set ourselves up for the rest of our lives."

"OK, that sounds reasonable. Now when the ambassador gets here, let me do all the talking. This has the potential to be a serious diplomatic incident right at the time when publicly Egypt and the UK are the best of allies, following the Gulf

War. I want to come to a compromise that everyone can walk away with a smile on their face. That might mean, Glenn, you might not get to keep the gold but right now let's not consider that. I am guessing your number one priority is the same as mine and that's to stop the need for you to go back to Egypt and face any charges?"

"You are absolutely right there, sir, I can't tell you how much I don't want to do that right now," said Glenn.

"Good enough then, that's our first priority then." He turned to the Professor. "Professor, I know you and the museum have put up a substantial amount of money to buy the coins, but do you think there may be a compromise to be had with the Egyptians?"

"Well, we are very happy to negotiate. I would love the coins to be on display in the museum, but we have to accept there are an awful lot of them and we would be happy to just have some of them on display. They are very rare so a real addition to our collection," said the professor. "However, the Egyptians, quite rightly in my opinion, are very defensive when it comes to precious artefacts leaving their country without permission. The antiquity laws were changed to stop this happening, so it won't be easy to get a compromise where we get to keep the coins."

"That's good background, Professor, it may well be that we have to use the number of coins as a bargaining position. Alright, everyone ready?" he said looking round the table.

Everyone nodded and Williamson and Amelia stood up to leave as they wouldn't be part of the meeting. Williamson gathered in the plates and cups, stacked them on the trolley and left the room. The three of them sat there in silence while the detective inspector made more notes in his notebook. Some time passed before there was a knock at the door and Williamson entered introducing the ambassador and his deputy.

Chapter 51

They entered gracefully, dressed in very smart three-piece suits and shook hands with everyone present. Glenn thought they looked like royalty and were obviously used to strutting around representing their country. Inspector Evans introduced the meeting and set the scene for the agenda before handing over to the ambassador.

"We, in the Egyptian government, are very unhappy with this situation. We have laws in place over many years to stop our precious antiquities being plundered from our country and dispersed around the world never to be seen again. These precious artefacts are the belongings of the Egyptian people and should be on display in Egypt. They are our history and we believe Mr Mulligan and his brother have flouted these laws and we want them to stand trial for their crimes. They deliberately came to Egypt with the purpose of stealing the coins and bringing them back to sell for their own gain! They are criminals and we insist justice is done." He became louder and louder throughout his speech and sat back looking to Glenn for a response.

Glenn was speechless and just stared at the ambassador. He was thinking, *Oh my god, I hadn't realised how serious this was. I am in real trouble here.* He was glad when the professor broke the silence, "I can assure you, Mr Ambassador, that Mr Mulligan and his brother were not aware of any such antiquity laws and in fact are very naïve in this complicated field. As soon as they had the chance, they came to me as the renowned expert in the UK and I have been able to help and guide them as we have gone along. As per procedure, I followed the law and let your people know of the find. We have done this many times before and have always come to a satisfactory conclusion."

He carried on, "They are certainly not criminals and were simply following a dying request from their beloved Granddad. And let's not forget if it wasn't for the three generations of Mulligans dating as far back as 1942, the coins would have been stolen by the Nazi's and definitely would never have been seen again."

Glenn was thinking, *Get in there, Professor!* He felt like the professor was fighting for Glenn's life.

"You make a good point, Professor, but it doesn't hide the fact that these men broke the international law and should be investigated appropriately," replied the Ambassador.

The inspector stepped in here, "Mr Ambassador, could I ask what the outcome is your government are looking for out of this episode?"

"We want justice and we want the coins returning to their rightful place in Egypt."

"And by justice, what would that look like?"

"We want the Mulligan brothers extraditing to Egypt to face trial of theft of the coins. There is also the other issue they need to be questioned about and that is the murder of two Egyptian citizens in the area of Egypt at the time of their visit," said the ambassador.

"Murder!" exclaimed Glenn, trying to put as much incredulity into the short statement. "Where did this happen, we just went over there, collected the coins and came home. Nothing more. We might have broken a law, but we didn't know anything about any antiquity laws, it never crossed our mind."

"Two Egyptian citizens were found dead at the foot of Mount Himeimat, which is not much further than thirty miles from El Alamein where you claim to be and two hundred miles from Cairo," said the ambassador.

"Two hundred miles, that's like from here to Manchester. You can't say that has anything to do with us," said Glenn.

"And with all respect, Mr Ambassador, there are over two thousand murders per year in Egypt, so statistically there was always going to be murders while the boys were visiting your country. I think it is a bit far-fetched to be looking at two young lads from the UK as your prime suspects," said the DI.

"Questions still need to be answered and there's still the theft of Egyptian treasures!" said the ambassador.

"OK, let's just try and calm down a little. We, the UK government and strong allies and friends to the Egyptian government, want to come to a suitable solution here but we cannot, and will not, support the extradition of two of our citizens on this matter," said the inspector. "There must be a compromise where everyone can walk away from this, celebrating the recovery of such a fantastic piece of Egyptian history and recognising the Mulligan's part in their recovery."

"What do you have in mind, Inspector?" said the ambassador who seemed to have calmed down.

"Well," he said, looking at the professor and Glenn, "we agree the coins should be returned to Egypt but that the Egyptian government should be rewarding Mr Mulligan rather than trying to throw him in jail."

"We are also grateful for the recovery of the coins and acknowledge the special relationship with our allies in the UK. Laws have been broken though and we can't be seen by the world to allow that to go unpunished," said the ambassador.

"No, precisely and we understand that position, Mr Ambassador, but celebrating the return of the coins and applauding the co-operation between our two countries must surely be seen as a satisfactory outcome. Certainly, I can say with confidence that it would be by the UK government. No one outside this room needs to know the coins left Egypt and that would also keep the integrity of the antiquity laws," said the inspector.

The ambassador stood up followed by his deputy who hadn't said a word in the meeting. "I will go and speak to my colleagues back in Egypt and meet you back in here at the same time tomorrow to discuss this further. Would that be acceptable to the UK government?"

"That certainly would, Mr Ambassador," said the inspector. He stood and shook his hand. The ambassador nodded to the professor and Glenn and left the room. The inspector and the deputy followed him out.

"Oh my god," sighed Glenn and put his head in his hands. "Thanks, Professor, for sticking up for me."

"No problem, Mr Mulligan, it had to be said. If I was reading his reactions right there, I think they will back down if we give them the coins. It will mean though giving your fortune up with it."

"No problem with me, sir, I just don't want to go back to Egypt!"

The inspector re-entered the room with Williamson and a worried-looking Amelia behind him. They all sat down, and he summarised the meeting, so everyone knew where they stood. "So, we cannot do anything else until tomorrow's meeting. Mr Mulligan, Williamson will run you to your hotel where you need to be confined to your room until tomorrow lunchtime when he will pick you up. Order room service but don't leave your room. I don't want you wondering around London. Let's hope we can nail a deal tomorrow. If I was a betting man, and I am not, I would say they are up for doing a deal but let's not count our chickens just yet!"

"Inspector, can I ask what happens if they don't do a deal?" said Glenn.

"Not something we want to think about, Mr Mulligan, but if they insist on extradition, then we may face months of court case battles ahead of us!"

Chapter 52

Glenn lay on the bed in the hotel room thinking through the events of the meeting. Did he feel confident about how it turned out? He couldn't make his mind up. At one point, the ambassador looked like he was going to drag him off to Egypt there and then but by the end of the meeting, he had calmed down and the inspector sounded confident. It looked like their fortune had gone up in smoke but right now, he just wanted to go back home and back to a normal life. Well, as normal as it could be keeping Amelia in it!

He looked at the clock, just after six he had better ring Brian and give him an update. He picked up the phone and dialled. Brian picked up he must have been sat by the phone waiting for the call. "How did it go, mate? Have you been arrested and thrown in the cells yet?" he said.

"Don't even joke, mate, it was an absolute nightmare. The Egyptian guy was spitting mad. Thought he was going to drag me off to Egypt there and then. I can tell you my arse was twitching big time. The professor and a Detective Inspector Evans were in there with me and they put up a great fight for us."

"Bloody hell, mate, sounds like it was horrendous. Are you OK?"

"Yeah I am OK; now I am back at the hotel. Under house arrest if you like, I am not allowed out so a long boring night ahead staring at the wall."

"Right. Where are we now then?"

"Well, the Egyptian guy mentioned the murders at Mount Himeimat. My heart skipped a beat, but I think the inspector diverted the conversation away from that. The ambassador stated he wanted the coins and he wanted us to go back and face charges for theft and to answer questions on the murders. The inspector said no way were the British government going to allow that. I tell you, Brian, I could have kissed him at that point!"

"Flippin' heck, so he was serious then?"

"Too right he was. Shouting and all sorts of things. I just tried to keep as quiet as I could. Anyhow, by the end, the inspector got him to admit that the outcome they really wanted was the coins back in Egypt as per the law. I think it would set a precedent if they didn't get the gold back."

"So where are our coins right now?"

"The police have them locked up in Scotland Yard. To be honest, mate, I think we have lost our fortune but right now, I

301

will do anything not to go back to Egypt and face any charges."

"Agree with you there, Glenn, we just really want this to go away. So, what happens now?"

"We have another meeting with the Egyptians tomorrow. They said they would go and speak to the bosses in Egypt and come back to us tomorrow with an offer. The inspector was confident we would get a deal, but it would probably mean giving up the coins."

"Oh well, it was a hell of an adventure and I think Granddad would have been proud of us. Let's see what they say then. Good luck, Glenn, when will you be home?"

"Well, I don't know to be honest. If I get out of there, then I will be heading north as soon as I can I tell you. If they want to push the extradition stuff, then the inspector said we could have months of court cases ahead. God knows what they will mean. Anyhow, I will give you a ring tomorrow either way at work."

They hung up the phone. Glenn lay back down on the bed thinking about all the possibilities. He felt hungry so started to look through the room service menu. There was a knock at the door, he got up and answered it. Amelia stood there. "Inspector Evans said you weren't allowed to leave your room, but he didn't say you couldn't have a visitor," she said.

Glenn stood to one side with a big smile on his face to allow Amelia past. She was wearing black leather trousers and high heels and a fluffy white cardigan which was off her shoulders showing some skin. She had her hair in a ponytail and looked amazing. She carried two bags, a shopping bag and an overnight bag by the looks of it.

"I thought you might like some goodies to eat and drink, so I called in at Marks & Spencer's and picked up some nice treats and a couple of bottles of red wine. You do like red wine, don't you?"

"Love it. This is fantastic, Amelia, thanks so much. I thought I was going to have a lonely boring evening on my own." He went across and kissed her and sat on the bed.

"I told my parents I was going to an all-night party so not to expect me home," she said.

"Oh right, what time to do you to leave?" said Glenn, sounding a little disappointed.

Amelia smiled at Glenn and then turned and walked to the door. She opened it and put the 'Do Not Disturb' sign on the outside of the handle. She closed and locked the door and turned back to Glenn. "I don't have to go, silly, that's what I told my parents. I was hoping you would keep me occupied all night." She walked back into the room unbuttoning her cardigan slowly.

Glenn sat on the bed with his mouth gaping open and Amelia couldn't help but laugh.

Chapter 53

Glenn sat at the conference table again with the professor and Detective Inspector Evans. He couldn't stop smiling, thinking back to the night before. The best night of his life he thought. He just needed to get out of here in one piece and life would be fantastic. Yes, he looked like losing his fortune, but he had gained Amelia and that was worth more than any mountain bag of gold.

"You look remarkably cheery considering the circumstances, Mr Mulligan," said the inspector.

"Just want to get this all over and done with, Inspector. That Egyptian fellow wasn't half angry yesterday and that really worries me. I am more than happy to give the coins up if he drops all the charges against me and my brother."

"Yes, that's exactly what we want as well, although don't forget you went to a lot of trouble to get those coins back and if it wasn't for you and your Granddad they may never have been found again. Lost to the world. I think that point landed with the ambassador," said the professor.

"I have spoken to the foreign office and they don't want any bad publicity out of this and anything that might stain the relationship between Britain and Egypt. They have had several calls with their counterparts in Egypt yesterday. The pressure is on for them to drop the extradition claims, so I am looking forward to their approach today," said the inspector. "Fingers crossed it goes our way. Leave all the talking to me unless absolutely necessary and if it is, I will ask you specifically to comment. OK?"

"Yes understood," said Glenn.

A few minutes later, there was a knock at the door and Williamson led the Egyptian delegation in from yesterday. They greeted everyone in the room with handshakes and sat down at the table. The ambassador had a folder and a stack of papers with him. Glenn couldn't help wondering was that some kind of charge sheet or formal demand to extradite him back to Egypt. The inspector kicked off the meeting by summarising what was discussed yesterday and then handing the floor to the ambassador.

"Thank you, Inspector. As you so eloquently stated, we were at an impasse yesterday but we, in the Egyptian government, are keen to work with our valued allies and come up with a suitable solution for this situation. It would be bad for both of our countries if this were played out publicly in the papers and on the news. I spent the evening on a conference call with the president and some of his key advisors and he agrees with my suggestion that we need to come to a satisfactory compromise here. The president had also spoken several times to your foreign minister and was, therefore, very well briefed."

Glenn was thinking, *This guy is really building his part. Did he really talk to the president or is he just full of himself? Surely, a president of a country wasn't talking about him. And what did he mean his idea to compromise the Inspector came up with that idea.*

The ambassador continued, "As you are aware, we have strict antiquity laws in place to stop this kind of thing happening. For decades, valuable pieces of Egyptian history were simply ripped out of our country and taken abroad. Stolen from the people and there was nothing we could do about it. Well, now there is under international law. We simply cannot let that happen. Egyptian history is one of the most fascinating and oldest in the world and we must preserve its integrity."

"Quite right," agreed the professor.

"We absolutely must have those coins returned to Egypt where they belong and can be displayed to the people. That is our highest priority and, therefore, we must look to agree a solution that makes this happen." He looked around the room and everyone nodded at his suggestion.

"I also noted from the conversations yesterday that Mr Mulligan was just trying to do the right thing and wasn't aware he was breaking the law. I explained this to the president and emphasised the fact that if it wasn't for the Mulligan family, these Egyptian treasures would have been lost forever."

"Thank you, Mr Ambassador, that is really appreciated," said the inspector.

"The president values his close relationship with the British people and, therefore, he has authorised me to make the following offer."

Here it comes, thought Glenn. *Do I walk out of here or is it going to be a nightmare?* The ambassador shuffled his papers and looked around the room with a dramatic pause. He really knew how to play his part as the man in control.

"In exchange for all three hundred and fifty coins. I have a document here that we would like signed by the professor on behalf of the British Museum and Mr Mulligan on behalf of his family, declaring full ownership to the Egyptian people and that they have no claim on the coins." He paused again looking around the room. "We would then be happy to drop all claims for extradition on Mr Mulligan and his brother."

Glenn's heart skipped a beat. He had lost his fortune as expected but he wasn't going to Egypt and that was a result.

The ambassador continued, "In a further gesture of good will from the Egyptian people we would like to offer Mr

Mulligan an award of a finder's fee of fifty thousand British pounds." He smiled this time as he looked around the room.

"That seems a very generous offer, Mr Ambassador, and I am sure the professor and Mr Mulligan will consider it most positively," said the inspector. He looked at Glenn and the professor. "Would you gentlemen like some time to consider the ambassador's generous offer."

Glenn was amazed. Had he heard that right? He was not going to Egypt, which was great, but they were also offering him fifty thousand pounds. This was a fantastic outcome. In his wildest dreams, he couldn't have hoped for this during the first exchanges of the meeting yesterday.

The professor spoke first while Glenn was still thinking about his good luck. "We are obviously very disappointed not to be able to display the coins in the museum, Mr Ambassador, but in light of the conversations over the last week, I think it is right and proper that they should reside in Egypt. However, we would be delighted to host an exhibition of the coins in the future if the Egyptian government would like to loan some of them to the British Museum."

"A kind offer, Professor, and I shall be glad to pass that onto my colleagues at the Museum of Egyptian antiquities in Cairo. Perhaps you would honour us with your presence when we launch the collection?"

"I would be absolutely delighted," said the professor.

They all looked round at Glenn. "Where do I sign?" said Glenn clapping his hands and there was an outburst of laughter around the room.

"I think that's a yes to your kind offer, Mr Ambassador," said the inspector.

Epilogue

It was a beautiful clear crisp late summer's day as the boys sat on the bench next to Granddad Victor's headstone. It was twelve months to the day since he had passed, and it felt right that the two boys spent some time with him. They were both handling their Egyptian gold coins twinkling in the sunshine. The deal struck with the Egyptians specifically stated three hundred and fifty coins and only the boys and the professor knew that there were two more. The professor never mentioned the two additional coins although he did give Glenn a knowing look when they had parted in London.

Amelia had seen Glenn off at the station and their long-distance relationship was still going strong. Glenn had even spent time in the Hollands Park family home which couldn't have been any different from his own. But her family had been very welcoming, and he loved going down to spend time in London with them and allowing Amelia to excitedly show him the sites of the capital.

The boys had decided to pool their money and buy a joint bachelor pad. They had recently moved in and were enjoying the freedom of no parents and no mortgage. They had had to go back to their jobs but on the whole, life was pretty good.

"Well, Granddad," said Glenn after a few minutes of silent reflection. "You really did set up the adventure of a lifetime for us, but we shouldn't have been surprised. I wish I had known you, Frank and Micky back then in the war. Those adventures you wrote about were amazing."

"Yeah and the treasure hunt you set up for us changed our life. Who would have thought between the three of us, we would have wrestled that gold from the Germans and fifty years later, got it back to the Britain?" said Brian.

"Only to give it back to the Egyptians, Granddad," said Glenn.

"For a small finder's fee, Glenn, don't forget."

"Yeah fifty grand, Hey Victor, what about that. If he is up there watching us, Brian, he must be laughing his head off with the outcome. We certainly got lucky in the end."

"We did, Glenn, although we can strike a return to Egypt off our future plans. I don't fancy going back just in case there is a file somewhere with our names on it."

"Looking back now, I just wish we had spent more time with him. Chance for him to tell us about his adventures. I would have loved to have heard them as he would have told it."

"It just didn't work out that way, mate. No point beating yourself up about it now. Come on, let's get back."

"You're right, mate. OK, Granddad we are off. See you soon and thanks for everything."

They got up from the bench and started the thirty-minute stroll home. It was such a lovely day that they had decided to walk. Glenn opened the front door and picked up the mail on the way in. He made his way through to the kitchen and put the kettle on and sat at the kitchen table looking through the letters. Mostly normal bills but this letter looked interesting. It had the date written in the top left corner, was handwritten and felt like it had a thick A4 pad inside. He opened it.

Hi Glenn, it's your Granddad here. If you are reading this then it's a year to the day since I died, and it's probably given you the fright of your life! How did you find the story I left you of the war? I hope you followed it up for me and you found the gold!! But if you think that was an adventure wait til you read about this one…………

"Brian, you're never going to believe this," he shouted.

The End